872-0661 Ave

TO JAMIE

FROM MUM
+ DAD

1972

WHITMAN

ALGONQUIN

ALGONQUIN
The Story of a Great Dog

by DION HENDERSON

Illustrated by DAVID STONE

® A WHITMAN BOOK

Western Publishing Company, Inc.
Racine, Wisconsin

"*Who knoweth the spirit of man that goeth upward, And the spirit of the beast that goeth downward to the earth?*"

I

Nothing else is left. I was very young when they were very old, but I remember how it was: the glistening white drives, the stables, the kennels, and the big house, with its wall of little windows. Thunder Hill, they called it; now hardly anyone remembers. The ruins are almost lost in the under-brush, but the stone is there, the stone and the word that will last as long as the stone lasts. It is the good marble like you buy your kinsmen, still gleaming smooth and veined the way it did when they had it carried from Italy, for the man who carved angels to come and cut upon it the word that was a name: ALGONQUIN.

A dog was called by that name, and nothing else remains. But I will tell you a true thing right at the beginning: There never was a dog like Algonquin.

1

MR. WASHINGTON WAS WAITING for us when they stopped the train at the Junction. I helped him get the bags, and Grandsir walked along the platform, stretching his legs. The station agent came out and said, "Evening, Colonel," as though Grandsir arrived at the Junction once a day instead of once a year.

"Evening, John," Grandsir said. "How are the birds this year?"

The station agent shook his head sadly. "Not many left, Colonel," he said. He always said that, and he always called Grandsir "Colonel." So did a lot of people at the Junction. He wasn't a colonel.

Mr. Washington told me they called him that because Grandsir hadn't spent much time here when he was young, and now he was so old he looked the way they remembered his daddy. That sounded very reasonable, except for one thing: His daddy wasn't a colonel, either. Grandsir's daddy was a major general and had his picture hanging in the library, with a saber under it, but I decided not to mention that part.

I liked Mr. Washington. He was a stooped, hollow-looking kind of a man, like maybe he had been left out in the sun too long and dried out. Although he did not exactly have whiskers, he did not exactly not have them, either, which puzzled me until I found out he shaved with scissors. But he could swear in the Chippewa language and chewed plug tobacco, and besides these two points in his favor, as far as I was concerned, he was a splendid hand with the dogs.

He had the trap to take us out to Thunder Hill, because in those days, whenever the creek was a little high, there wasn't a bridge over it, and sometimes they did not get the bridge up again until it was time for the creek to have another flood. You could ford the creek in a rig, and driving a horse was part of the dividend I got.

It was fall, and most of the way the road wound

through the hardwood ridges and the high marshes, where cold, fast streams got their start. The way the trees burned in the sun, with the red of sumac and the flare of goldenrod and the intense blue patches of field aster on the slopes, it did not matter how long the drive took. Every once in a while, we would go around a curve and there would be a burst of alarm from one of the roadside dusting places, and a partridge would whir away through the bright leaves, and once we saw a cock pheasant, all green and scarlet and chocolate, swaggering unhurriedly into the weeds. That was the first pheasant I ever saw loose like that, and I was very excited.

But Mr. Washington made a mark in the air with his finger.

"Fine feathers don't make fine birds," he said. "Nothing but spaniel birds."

That was about as harsh a thing as Mr. Washington could say. He meant that you could hunt pheasants with spaniels, and Mr. Washington felt that any bird you didn't hunt exclusively with pointing dogs was unfit to associate with gentlefolk.

I started to ask a lot of questions, but there wasn't time. We broke out of the wooded ridges onto the edge of the high prairie and began to climb toward Thunder Hill. The red road made a long curve upward, and the double row of white cedars came to meet it. Where the cedars began, the road stopped being red and was made of little white stones that glistened, and the horses stepped more springily until the drive swept around and leveled off in front of the big house. It was set up there with the great, gnarled old bur oaks around it, and Grandsir said, "Those oaks haven't changed much since I was a boy. They were the real pioneers; they broke the sod and stopped the fire that kept making more prairie."

Even over the sound of the hooves and wheels crunching on the stones, I thought I could hear dogs barking.

But to Grandsir I said, "Yes, sir."

"A man can read the history of the land in the pedigree of a bur oak," Grandsir said. "It is a lot more interesting and accurate history than some that are substituted in books."

"Yes, sir," I said doggedly, straining my ears for the dog noises and beginning to form a strong feeling about oaks in general and bur oaks in particular.

"Maybe you'd like to learn about oaks," Grandsir said relentlessly.

"Yes, sir," I said. "Maybe when I am a little older."

Then he chuckled, and I knew he had been fooling, because he knew what I was listening for, too.

When the rig pulled up in front of the big house, Uncle Ovid came out on the porch and started down the steps, and the excitement that had been building up in me almost hurt, because I could hear the dogs, all right. Still, I knew enough to mind my manners.

I stood aside, and Grandsir shook hands formally with Uncle Ovid, and they exchanged concern for each other's health. Uncle Ovid was Grandsir's brother. They looked quite a lot alike and acted some alike and quarreled nearly all the time they were together, but you got the idea they wouldn't have given up getting together for anything.

Grandma said the good Lord had given them both the same material to work with, and they started out to make themselves into the same kind of men, and Uncle Ovid started all the things Grandsir did, but while Grandsir finished them, Uncle Ovid had to stop and go out and look after the puppies at critical moments, so he never amounted to much.

Where Grandsir was tall and formal and austere in black broadcloth and a black string necktie and looked like a poet—which he wasn't—or a judge, which he was, Uncle Ovid just barely managed to look presentable, and maybe a little on the rakish side of that. He had white side-whiskers that were very white all the way and a white moustache that was a little tobacco-colored around the edges, which Grandma said was an affectation because Uncle Ovid thought it made him look like a heck of a fellow.

Finally, there on the porch of the big house, Uncle Ovid turned and looked at me and appeared astonished that I had shown up.

"Well, I declare," he said.

I took his hand and said, "How do you do, sir?"

Uncle Ovid shook my hand quite a while, then allowed he was purely glad to see me. All the time I could hear the dogs, plainer and plainer.

"Did you have a comfortable trip, boy?" Uncle Ovid was very solicitous.

"Yes, sir," I said. "Oh, my goodness, yes."

Uncle Ovid turned then, to wink at Grandsir, and before he could turn back, I was gone.

I sneaked around the corner of the big house and got the summer arbor between me and the corner, and then I really dug out. The big house was right up on the edge of the hill, where it looked over everything. I ran along the path that went behind it and past the summer arbor and the back gardens, and where the path forked, with one going down to the stables, I took the other one.

There was a special clearing for the kennel house. It was set back, with a double row of evergreens shielding the north and west sides, but the other sides were opened for the winter sun. The kennel was a low white frame building divided off into compartments, and the runs came out separately on the south side, with another separate guard fence that went around them all, so just in case a dog got out of his run, he was held by the second fence. You find some awful fence busters among pointers. There was a gate in the outer fence, but it was locked, and there was a door into the kennel house, but it was locked, too.

The dogs came out in their runs, barking a little

19

but mostly talking to me, the way bird dogs do when they have been handled a good deal and seen different people and liked the people they knew. Indian Maid was the first one. She was the one I really wanted to see, except for the puppies.

She was a fine dog, and she sort of whistled because she wanted to get to me as badly as I wanted to get to her, but there were the two fences. I got down on my hands and knees and worked one arm through the links on my side, and Indian Maid tried to get her nose through hers, but her muzzle was too big, so she put her foot through, and even then the space was so wide we could barely shake hands.

I didn't hear anybody coming until Grandsir said, very close behind me, "You'd think the boy kind of wanted to get at the dogs, Ovid."

And Uncle Ovid said, gentle-like, "I declare, I don't think I ought to have teased the boy that way, delaying him."

I worked my arm out of the wire and felt sheepish because I was blushing to be caught that way. Indian Maid stood up on the wire and hollered a little about my taking my hand back on my own

20

side of the fence. That brought the puppies out.

They were in the next run, that really was part of the same run but was separated by a two-foot fence, so the Maid could go back and forth if she wanted to, but the puppies couldn't follow her. It was the same way inside the house, even though the puppies were three months old and weaned long ago. Sometimes you have to do that with a bitch if she is the kind that worries about her puppies as long as she knows they are around.

Now, with all eight of them out in the run, they looked about four times as big as they should have. I had been busy remembering just how they looked when they were getting their eyes open. For a moment I despaired of trying to sort them all out again and find individuals. They all looked alike.

All but one. The reason I couldn't find him in that big-footed, ear-flapping, tail-wagging storm was that he wasn't there. The others were out bouncing against the wire and yelping, and then he came to the door of the house and walked deliberately down the incline and looked at me—he and I, all alone: Algonquin.

He was white in the body—not a dark hair, all

white to the ears—and his head was solid liver. The head was what you noticed, from the time he was born. You felt somehow, long before you could really tell, that there would be clean, harsh, predatory lines about it. It reminded you a little of a baby eagle, but different—or a young king, but different —of many things, but always different, different. Maybe it was his eyes, a little cloudy and undecided, as though he did not know whether he would love greatly or hate bitterly. His eyes might be yellow, when he knew what he had to know.

Grandsir cleared his throat and startled me so I jumped, because I had forgotten all about everyone else.

"Well," he said, "have you changed your mind?"

"No, sir," I said. "That's my dog."

"The boy's got his rights," Uncle Ovid said.

"Never mind." Grandsir did not want to spoil any of this for me. "We have been over all this before."

I didn't understand exactly what they had been over, but they had been over it, all right. They both saw something in my puppy, and what they saw made Uncle Ovid smile happily and made Grand-

22

sir's mouth go shut like a trap. A mysterious dispute had gone on, from the time Maid's litter was born until I picked the pup with the strange dark head.

After that, Grandsir had said, "There is one more thing you want to remember about dogs, boy, and the glory of achievement and the lasting quality of renown: You want to remember that the most famous dog of all had three heads."

I was astonished. "What was his name?" I asked.

Grandsir said, "Cerberus."

"I never heard of him," I said.

"Well—" Grandsir smiled a little—"after all, he wasn't a bird dog. He was sort of a retriever."

You can see that Grandsir did not really hold it against me that I was so young. We had a splendid relationship, but sometimes our serious conversations, like the one about Cerberus, became very desperate, from my viewpoint, because Grandsir would say things to me that I couldn't possibly figure out for another twenty-five years. I worried a good deal about my density, until Grandma told me one time it was all right, because Grandsir occasionally told grown-ups things they wouldn't figure out if they lived to be a hundred.

Anyway, down there at the kennel run, when I saw Algonquin again, I did not want to leave him, even overnight. He did not want me to go, either, but there was no way a puppy or a boy could make grown-ups understand. Mr. Washington came down to feed the dogs and lock them in for the night, but Algonquin wouldn't enter the kennel door, and Mr. Washington had to crawl out and catch him, and when we had walked up the path almost to the big house, we still could hear a puppy voice raised in lament—strange and wild and not like a puppy at all.

All through supper, for no reason, I kept feeling as though I wanted to cry, and when we had finished eating, Grandsir looked at me carefully and said that the trip had sort of tired him out, and he thought maybe he'd go to bed early. I said I thought maybe I would, too.

When Grandsir and Uncle Ovid were boys, they had eleven brothers and sisters, and there was room for all of them in the big house. Now, even when we were visiting, that made only five people staying in it, counting Mr. Washington and his wife, who did the cooking, at least part of the time. Most

of the rooms that were upstairs hadn't been opened for years, and I always had a big bedroom to myself.

Each year when I went into it, I knew no one had been in it since I left, except Mr. Washington, to get it ready for me. It was always damp and strange but still a little familiar, like a place you have dreamed about, and, although I did not really know where things were, if I did not think but just acted, I could find everything without any trouble. It felt kind of spooky, knowing all about a place I couldn't remember on purpose.

There was a big brass bed with posts on it and curtains hanging all around it, and there was a bureau with a washbasin big enough to take a bath in and a pitcher that always seemed to be full of ice water. The bed was cold, and on one side was another dish, with roses and cherubs on it, and I want to tell you that was cold, too. If there is a common denominator that establishes a universal meeting ground among people who have followed the dogs all their lives, it likely is the recollection of there always being something cold on which to sit. Each place was colder than the last one, despite the laws of chance and circumstance. You ask anybody, and you'll find it was always so.

That night I crawled, shaking, between the stiff, cold sheets, trying to take up as little room as possible, and it seemed like it never would get warm in there. In the morning it would be the other way around: It would be nice and warm in bed, but you could see your breath in the room outside the bed, and you stayed until the smell of bacon and wheat cakes coming up the stairs hauled you unwillingly out of the cocoon. You can get very nostalgic about things like that afterward, but at the time, it was difficult to be objective.

Presently it was warm in bed, and I drowsed luxuriously, not quite asleep, thinking about the puppy and the way he seemed to be set apart from the others and the way I could not help picking him and the different things he made Grandsir and Uncle Ovid feel. I thought of how he would grow up—Algonquin, great and famous—and the dream grew; he stalked through the dream, so real that there wasn't the slightest doubt in my mind what he would be. I was so sure, in the dream that night, that I was not surprised at all by the way it worked

27

out later. The dream was full of splendor and of triumph, and I knew he would be a great dog, even though I wasn't sure what a great dog was, and I wanted to put my hands out and touch him, but I couldn't do it. He wasn't there, although I could see him. He wasn't really there at all, and it frightened me so I woke.

The bedroom was dark but not regular black dark. It was sort of reddish dark, and when I pushed open the curtains, I could see the red light mixing in with the dark and changing and growing stronger. I did not know where I was or what was happening, and I hollered good and loud. But no one answered. The dream had frightened me a good deal, and now I scrambled out of bed in complete panic and ran downstairs, but no one was there, either. Then I had to run back up alone in the empty reddish dark to get my clothes, then back down again, but by that time I was awake enough to know there was a fire.

Outside, you could see fire reflected everywhere, from the trees and glinting on the walks, but I could not see the fire itself. I started running down the path, and a man running toward me saw where

I was just in time to pick me up. The man was Mr. Washington.

"What is it?" I asked. "What's happening?"

"Nothing you can do, boy." Mr. Washington's voice was deep and calm. "Like the Book says, old world is going up in flames."

It turned out to be true, in a manner of speaking. Mr. Washington's world was going up in flames. The fire was in the kennel, and all the dogs were locked inside.

2

THEY KEPT TRYING to do things, even after they knew nothing could be done. There were quite a few people. Thunder Hill being so high, neighbors could see the fire for miles. Two men were working on the gate of the big fence. One of them held a bar, and the other swung a big hammer, even though Uncle Ovid was there and had the key in his pocket. No one thought to ask him. When they had that lock off, there would be another one on the run fences, and taking that off, too, wouldn't help, anyway, because the dogs all were inside for the night, and the drops were down so they couldn't get out into the runways. No one thought of that, either.

But it happened that the one swinging the hammer slipped, and the one holding the bar had his hand all mashed, and the bones stuck out of it so he couldn't hold the bar anymore, and no one else would do it, so they didn't even get through the first fence.

The flickering red light of the fire lighted up the trees above, and some of the bur oaks that hold their leaves so long after they are dry were illuminated, and once or twice leaves caught fire and burned without any flames, just glowing red sparks eating into them, the way oak leaves burn, and one of the men had to go back to the big house and sit out on the roof with a wet mop, to watch for the sparks.

The fire must have started in the room where they mixed the feed and stored tackle, right behind the door, because when Uncle Ovid first got there, he unlocked the kennel door and opened it and the flames whooshed out, so he slammed it shut again.

Mr. Washington put me down and went back to the fire, and I followed along because there wasn't anything else to do. The fire was through the roof and that whole side of the building by then, making the light, and was just going through the hallway that led past all the pens. I stood there, so scared that I didn't really understand what was happening, while the men ran back and forth, with the fire

31

glinting red off their sweaty faces, all shouting hoarsely, and Mr. Washington's wife worked with overalls over her nightgown and her hair up in curlers. She didn't shout or run around. She had a scrub bucket, and she would go to the well and pump the bucket full of water and carry it back and heave it into the fire, and the fire wouldn't show any sign of noticing it, but she would go back for another bucket.

I don't know what the dogs thought, but they were all good dogs, intelligent dogs, and they knew about pain and death in the way that any dog does after he has come to know people. They were locked in their little pens inside the building, and the fire ate its way to them and licked over them, and then Grandsir walked up to me and put a hand on my head.

His hand was very big and steady, and his face looked very old and tired but not surprised, as though he felt very bad about what was happening, but it was nothing new to him.

"I am glad you are very young, boy," he said quietly. "You will not remember too much about this. Nature is very wise that way, and it is a good thing, because a boy should not remember how it sounds when dogs or horses die in a fire."

They are not alike at first. The horses are very emotional, and they do not have much confidence in men to begin with. But dogs are very brave, and, in addition, they trust you, and that is the hardest part. The feeling of pain is a kind of luxury, and pointers have Spartan souls. In a fire, they sometimes talk very seriously, but then they are quiet until they begin to burn and the iron in them melts, and sometimes they are dead before it melts enough for them to scream.

Not always.

The fire must have reached some of the younger dogs just then, because I put my hands over my face, and Grandsir's big hand on my head was very heavy, but it still was steady.

"Not a boy or anyone," he said.

Then he took his hand off my head so suddenly I almost fell, and I heard him say in a great voice, *"Ovid!"*

And he went toward the kennel with long strides, and I started, blubbering, after him, but someone stopped me, and it was Mr. Washington. He was kneeling close enough so the fire made you all hot when it flared. Uncle Ovid was still closer. He had dressed, but he had been in the fire enough so that there were holes burned in his clothes, and his hair and moustache were black, and just when I looked at him, an ember landed in his beard and flared, and he reached up carelessly and crushed it out.

His hands were all black and he was carrying an ax, and Grandsir started to reach out for him but at the last minute shrugged and stood aside. A man does what he has to do.

Mr. Washington was mumbling something there beside me, and finally I understood what it was he was saying: "Now I lay me down to sleep, I pray the Lord my soul to keep," over and over again.

"Mr. Washington," I said, "that is not the kind of a prayer to be saying now."

But Mr. Washington looked at me quite calmly and said, "That is the prayer I know." And he kept on saying it.

Up there close, Uncle Ovid's face was strange and terrible. It was calm and the mouth was straight and the lines up under his moustache were straight, and he did not look like anything at all. I never had

34

seen anyone look like that before, but none of us had any trouble remembering how it was, because that is how he looked most always afterward.

With the fire licking out, almost touching him, his face did not change, and he swung the ax into the wall where Indian Maid's quarters were. He made a big hole, too, but before he could do any more, the fire came out at him, *whoosh,* and then suddenly, in the glare, we saw her, the Maid, burning all over but not paying any mind, picking up something and jumping right for the opening, where the flames were alive and boiling, but coming through all right at the very last—an indomitable dog in whom the fire could not melt the iron, could not even soften it, because when she landed, she was safe from all the fires that threaten the spirits of men and dogs all their lives. She landed all dead in a heap.

But what she carried rolled out ahead, smoking and singed but not hurt.

No one moved for a moment, just standing there with the shock and the weariness and all coming down on them together for that little while. Then the thing the Maid had been carrying got up on

35

unsteady legs and looked around and, with a lurch of strange decision, turned and started walking deliberately back toward the roaring flames.

Uncle Ovid jumped forward and caught it and picked it up and brushed off the sparks and carried it back. We edged up to look, but before I really saw, I knew suddenly how it was; I knew by the coldness that was inside me all the while and grew out all through me, despite the heat, so that I shivered and could not stop shivering, and my teeth rattled, and Mr. Washington put an arm around my shoulders.

He pointed to the puppy Uncle Ovid held.

"Poor little tyke," he said pityingly. "He don't know what he doing, there."

But the puppy's head was up, and the eyes looked at us from the dark mask—not afraid, not excited, not puzzled anymore, not anything, but reflecting the fire coldly, and strange, strange, strange.

That was Algonquin, and I tell you there never was a dog like Algonquin. I stood there, hearing the other dogs die and seeing the flames getting bigger and wilder. Mr. Washington repeated, in that singsong voice of lament, "Poor tyke, he don't know what he doing; no, he don't."

But he knew, all right. I knew he knew, and the strange, strange eyes looked at me and knew I knew —and knew also that I would never, never tell.

Grandsir took me away then and put me back to bed and talked to me awhile about the living and the dying you have to go through. There was no way to get away from those things, he said. Some people spend all their lives trying to get away from something, he said. It might be another kind of people, or the same kind, or a way of life. But no matter what it was, he said, the things they are trying to get away from really are the harsh realities of life and death, and you can't get away from these, so it is all for nothing.

Grandsir still was there when I went to sleep. It was nearly morning then, and I slept until late in the day. When I woke, the house was very quiet, and it did not seem possible that anything so terrible had happened overnight. But as soon as I started downstairs, I knew it had, all right, because the quiet in the house was the kind of quiet there is before a funeral. Of course, there was no funeral, not for many years, but the big house was full of the feeling, and it never quite went away, ever afterward.

For a moment I thought that if I went boldly outside and down the familiar path, the kennels would be there, just like they were the day before, and Indian Maid would come out and talk to me, and the puppies would bark, and the other dogs would come out and talk, too. But in the kitchen there was a box on the floor, and Algonquin was lying in the box, and when I saw him, I did not want to go outside anymore.

No one said very much. After supper we went out on the front porch, where the rockers were and where you could look away for miles in the dusk, across the wintering grounds and the marsh and the river and the thousands of acres of prairie that faded into the dark before you could see the far line of hills.

Presently it was full dark and quiet, except for the rockers creaking and night sounds far away. I sat on the steps. It was warm, almost like summer, except for the winy air, already cleared and sharpened by an early frost. It was warm enough to bring the fireflies back, and they swarmed down in the marsh so that, to us on the hill, it was like looking down on the stars, and it gave you a happy, uneasy feeling, but maybe only if you were a boy. Then if you looked up and saw the other stars, very big and cold because the sky was very black and close, you thought how the idea of two sets of stars in opposite places was like a lot of other things— one was real and one wasn't, but there really wasn't much point in worrying about them, because you weren't ever going to reach either one. A bat swooshed by the porch, felt but not seen, making a noise that really wasn't any noise but what you felt, and I started saying to myself what Grandma always said: "Bat, bat, come under my hat, and I'll give you a piece of bacon."

"Well, boy—" Uncle Ovid's voice was almost like Grandsir's, quieter and sort of brooding, and presently I understood it was because he was going back a long way in his mind for something—"well, boy, you have seen one of the great endings."

I sat still. From the other side of the porch, Grandsir said, "That is a true thing, Ovid, about your Maid. She was worthy of High Valor and Riptide and the rest."

That gave me a start. Those were familiar names of familiar dogs, familiar from the pictures in the library at home and from Grandma's talking about them. But I didn't recall that Grandsir had said very much about them, and he never had said anything whatever about how they died.

Uncle Ovid must have known what he meant, but he didn't give any sign. He had started out to talk to me, and he kept it up.

"Your first dog seems to live a long time, boy," he said. "Oh, yes, he seems to live a long time. Years don't mean much, and you'll find it out when you get enough on hand so you can really compare, but your first dog is with you during the important time, when you're changing and growing and learning so many wonderful things that later on are not so wonderful maybe, and though there aren't so many years involved, it seems you and him come a powerful long way together. You get real devoted, you and your first dog, if you're a proper man, and that's true even if you grow up enough to learn that your first dog isn't such a much of a dog."

Uncle Ovid paused momentarily and chuckled.

"And your own quality, too," he said. "That's kind of a delicate subject, but your first dog is too polite to let you know very much he finds out. He saves that for the later dogs, and they'll let you know, all right."

The rocker creaked a little. The next time it was Grandsir's voice, saying, "Your last dog is the same way, boy; he seems to live a long time, but it never is long enough, or else it is much too long. That is because the work he does is the last dog work you'll have of your own, but you have had so much of it during all the years that you are very critical, and that makes it hard for your last dog. If he is not very good, you become impatient and wish it were done with, but if it turns out he is good enough, then he is really good, and you know it and he knows it, and each day is harder to go through than the previous one because you know you are going together toward the very last time."

There was another little silence, and I certainly wasn't going to break it. I could feel chills on top of chills all over me, and my mouth was dry, and I tried desperately to keep track of what they were saying, because between them they knew more about bird dogs than most people suspected there was to know and some things not even the dogs had found out yet. A flare of light burst on the porch and nearly frightened me to death, but it was just Uncle Ovid lighting his pipe again. I understood suddenly how a gun-shy dog feels; even the match was more fire than I wanted.

But the next instant there was another sound on the porch: a dog walking. He came out of the house, stopped a moment, then advanced until I could feel him close and reached out to touch him.

Algonquin, attracted by something. I shuddered. Attracted by fire.

Grandsir stirred invisibly in the dark of the porch.

"Now, Ovid," he said, and his voice was a little hoarse, as though maybe he was catching cold. "Now, Ovid, it is your turn again."

Uncle Ovid did not say anything.

Grandsir said, "You, Ovid—you tell him about the great dogs now, and how you know them, and what makes them what they are, and for what."

The rocker stopped creaking and the puppy stopped walking, and the sudden silence nearly deafened me.

"You know I can't do that." Uncle Ovid's voice was strange, too. It sounded as though he had come

42

back from the places he had been remembering and was very tired. "It ain't proper to talk like that."

After a moment he added, "There ain't hardly anybody knows enough about God to say for sure all them things about a great dog."

"You and I." Grandsir was not catching cold, after all; it was the courtroom voice in which he summed up evidence that different people had different feelings about but couldn't change one way or another.

"I know enough, and I have saved something," he said. "You know enough, and all your life you could not bear to save anything."

I don't know how long it was before anyone moved after that. The puppy was sitting quietly near me, close enough to touch, but I didn't touch him. We sat there, maybe thinking the same things about each other, until I could not stand it any longer. I said good night and went upstairs, thinking how I never heard Grandsir say anything like that. But I never heard him say anything that wasn't a true thing in the way he meant it, not before and not afterward, so maybe it wasn't an untrue thing that time, either.

The next morning we were supposed to go home, and Mr. Washington had the rig ready, but Uncle Ovid was not around. I went out in back, not wanting to but knowing where he was, and there he was, all right, standing beside the ruins of the kennel. The timbers were all black and fallen in, and every once in a while a wisp of smoke would curl up from somewhere in the middle. What was worst, the fences still were standing, all double-locked and mouse-tight and backed up against nothing, just nothing. They would stay that way. I saw Uncle Ovid standing there, looking at the awful empty runs, and I knew that nothing ever would be behind the wire here again. He stood there, straight and braced, holding the puppy, and I thought that the puppy was getting pretty big to hold that way and was pretty big for the Maid to have carried, but she had carried him, all right. It was not until long afterward that I wondered how long Uncle Ovid had been standing there.

Mostly what I went back there for was the puppy, to get him and take him home to be my dog, the way a boy wants a dog. But when I saw him and saw the ruins, I knew all at once how ridiculous it was. He had not been saved from the fire to be a playmate for a little boy. Not for that, Indian Maid, with her hair burned off to her skin and the skin black where it was not burning with the oils in it, moving relentlessly through the flames because she could not die until she was done. Not for me.

I knew it suddenly and bitterly and burst into tears, and Uncle Ovid turned and asked gently, "What's the matter, boy?"

I shook my head. It would have been presumptuous for a boy to explain what no grown man has a right to understand.

"Will you take him now, boy?"

I shook my head again.

"Please, boy." Uncle Ovid was almost pleading. "You take him now."

"No, sir," I said. "He has to stay with you. You have to keep him and help him do whatever it is he has to do."

Uncle Ovid stood still for a moment. His face was as gray as the ashes.

"Well, boy," he said finally, "I guess none of us got much choice. I guess we do what we got to do, in the only way we can, and in the end we got nobody to blame but ourselves."

He looked back at the ruins and said, "I guess I got to do it one time more."

After a while I figured out that as far as he was concerned, I wasn't there anymore. I tiptoed away and left him stroking the dark head that was looking the same place he was looking, at the burned place, and beyond it, the dog whose name would be a word upon the stone: *Algonquin.*

3

THE DOGS THAT EVERYONE REMEMBERS all were gone, before my time, from the big brick house where I grew up. Grandsir had no dogs at all in my time. Once I asked him, and he turned and looked out the window and presently said he guessed maybe it was because he did not care so much for dogs anymore. But I had seen a little of the partly sad and partly angry expression on his face before he turned away, and I never asked him again.

Even so, there wasn't much chance of my growing up in ignorance. Our house was full of reminders of the great days and the great dogs and the names that were so famous you might have doubted they ever belonged to real times and places, except for the pictures.

In the library, the books went up higher than I

was, but above them were the pictures. They marched around the room in wide frames, the tall, splendid, high-stationed dogs, and over the mantel there was a life-sized painting of High Valor, with his wins engraved on a brass plate fastened to the frame. In bird dog field trials, they call any of the four placements in an Open-All-Age stake a win, but most of High Valor's were for first place, and three were championships. He was not the only one, either. The china closet was full of silver bowls and vases and trays that represented regional and national bird dog titles in the trials where the champion was the best of the very good and proved it face-to-face. The U.S. Chicken Championship and the National Free-for-All and the Stars and Stripes and the rest of them are not won against neighborhood dogs in backyard trials. Those are the big leagues, and in the old days, either you won there or you did not bother to win anywhere.

There never was any doubt in my mind about the dogs. I knew all about what I was going to do, without thinking very much about it. One time in school we were supposed to tell about what we were going to do when we grew up. The teacher looked very hard at me, and I had to say something pretty quick.

The kid across the aisle said someday he was going to have a million dollars, and the kid ahead of me said he was going to be a U.S. Senator.

I looked away from the teacher, who was not much to look at, even as teachers go, and blurted, "Someday I will have a puppy and he will become a famous champion and a U.S. Senator could not buy him for a million dollars."

The teacher didn't like it much. He wrote a note to Grandsir, and I took it home and stood there twisting my cap while Grandsir read it. He read it carefully and scowled and glared at me, then read it again and said by thunder, I'd better watch my *p*'s and *q*'s.

I was very worried, but Grandma took me aside later and explained that he really was very pleased but would not ever let me know. That was because he had been very disappointed in the way my daddy felt about the dogs, and he could not bear to be disappointed again, she said. My daddy had come

along at a very disappointing time, when everyone
was disappointing everyone else about everything,
and my daddy's not being around anymore when
everyone else got over it probably was what disappointed Grandsir most of all.

Still, after the teacher's note, I noticed Grandsir
watching me with a strange expression every once
in a while, and at last I asked him if I was in danger
of disappointing him, too.

"Boy—" you could tell from the mock sternness
that it was all right—"boy—" his thick gray eyebrows
wrenched themselves into a wry angle—"boy,"
he said, "I am very pessimistic about people in
general. Thus, although I am seldom confounded by
merit, I also am very rarely disappointed."

"It sounds sort of discouraging," I said.

"Oh, no," Grandsir said. "People are my pro-
fession. But it is a reason why I once thought very
highly of several dogs."

That was one of the things he said that confused
me, but when I took it up with Grandma, she said
there doubtless was a first-class philosophical prin-
ciple in it somewhere, and I was sure to find it

eventually, and when I did, I should let her know.

Anyway, nothing more was said, until one day Grandsir suggested I put on my boots in the morning, and when I asked why, he said because we were going to a field trial, naturally.

He did not give me any chance to become interested in mediocre dogs. The first trial I ever saw was a regional championship. Those are the trials that qualify dogs for the National Bird Dog Championship at Grand Junction, where only major champions are eligible to run and the splendid performances are what you have a right to expect.

Grandsir had me on the saddle in front of him, and when a brace of dogs was cast off, I turned and looked up at him questioningly, and he said yes, they were fine dogs. That happened several times; then I saw one that was different.

She was a tall white bitch with liver ears and a sprinkle of ticking on her forequarters, walking like she was all alone, and I felt goose bumps on my arm just from looking at her and turned to Grandsir, not questioning this time but with my eyes round and almost scared.

51

"That's the way it is, boy." Grandsir sounded immensely pleased about something. "If you have the feeling, no one needs to tell you what is a fine dog."

We were looking at Mary Montrose, who won the National before she was two years old and when she was done had won it three times.

After that I spent a good deal of time in the library. I sat there and looked at the pictures of the great dogs: High Valor and Riptide and Roanoke and Prime Minister. I looked at the beautifully angulated quarters and the short loins and the long, laid-back shoulders, where the secrets of a bird dog's running gear lie. I looked at the musculature, immensely compact and powerful, to resist fatigue, the rib cage deep and wedge-shaped, like a tall V, so that the forelegs could move in that great earth-devouring step-out, completely free of friction from the rigid skeletal frame. I looked at these things and memorized them.

And mostly I looked at the heads, at the shape and temper of the way they were held, because a dog is like a man: That is where he lives, and if the

dog who dwells there in that little space does not will strongly and unendingly for achievement, then all the rest is for nothing.

All the while the words that were names soaked into me—the names of dogs and men and the names of the far places like Hernando and Solon Springs and Shuqualak and Grand Junction and the prairie towns from Kansas to Saskatoon.

One day Grandsir passed in the hallway, then stopped abruptly and looked at me.

"If you keep studying, boy, you will know a fine dog every time."

"Yes, sir."

That, after all, was my intention. He stood very tall and stern in the doorway.

"And after that, you will be satisfied just to look at pictures and at other people's dogs?"

He was asking a question, all right.

I said, "No, sir."

"I see." Grandsir pulled at his jowl thoughtfully. He had a gaunt, distinguished face, but he was what they call a little throaty.

After a painful wait, I said, "Sir?"

"Nothing," Grandsir said. "I see. That's all."

And it was. Every once in a while it seemed to me that Grandsir was going to talk to me about what it would take to satisfy me, but at the last minute he would pause and scowl at me and pull his jowl, and I knew it would not be that time, either. I tried to find out from Grandma, but she just said it was because he was very critical himself, from having a hundred years or so of experience, and he likely did not want to spoil my taste. I could tell from the bantering way she said it I was not supposed to believe it, but there must have been some reason.

The nearest I came to getting a dog of my own, those days, was one time when a seedy-looking old man who, I overheard Grandma say, raised seven different kinds of hell and dropper pups back in the hills came in to thank Grandsir for not sending him to jail or something. A dropper is a crossbred pointer-setter and was very popular once with people who did not take time to figure out that they didn't have much chance of doing accidentally what the breeders of setters and the breeders of pointers were doing on purpose. But this old fellow had a puppy

55

in his arms, orange and white and pretty as anything to me, just because it was a real live bird dog, even though it had a butterfly nose.

The man still was on the steps, not even on the porch proper, when Grandsir opened the big front door and said sharply, "No, no, no, Albert."

Then he went quickly outside and shut the door firmly, almost on my nose, and presently the man went away, still carrying the puppy. Grandsir came back in, looking unhappy, and when he saw me standing there with my chin not very steady, he looked worse, but a little angry, too.

"Now, here is a true thing, boy," he said to me. "You do not want to acquire either the first puppy or the first woman you get a chance at, and for substantially the same reason. There is more to the respective subjects than you can learn by looking at pictures."

He hesitated, and his eyebrows slanted humorously, as though he were somewhat surprised at what he'd said. Then he added, "We admire them, boy, for the very qualities we cultivate ourselves and expect of one another."

56

"Which ones?" I asked. "The dogs or the women?"

"An excellent question," Grandsir said. "Oh, to be sure, an excellent question."

So you can see that Grandma was right about his being critical, but wrong about the other. He did not care one bit about spoiling my taste.

I guess he thought about it some, though, after that, because it was only a little while before he started talking about going to visit Uncle Ovid at the Old Place. Uncle Ovid had all the dogs that were left now, Grandma said. Once he and Grandsir both had the dogs, but then Grandsir gave up the dogs and got a big brick house in town and his name in the newspapers sometimes, Grandma said, and all Uncle Ovid had were a few dogs left, but lots of people who used to know them both thought Grandsir had died.

Now Uncle Ovid had another very fine dog. Her name was Indian Maid, and they said maybe she would be a little better than very fine, if nothing happened. She was a fall derby that year, not quite two years old, and eligible for most of the big

57

futurities, where you have to file an entry before your pups are born.

I liked Thunder Hill right away, and Uncle Ovid. It was like going home to someplace that you remembered a little vaguely, as though you had been gone a long while, but, of course, with me it was because I had heard so much about it at home. And Uncle Ovid had a way of talking to a boy in dead earnest, so that you knew it, despite the smile wrinkles around his eyes and the comical way his side-whiskers had of sticking out in different directions, from his stroking them uphill.

It does not matter much to a boy what is discussed on such occasions; a boy is a lot like a puppy that way—he is not very bright about details, but he is very good indeed at absorbing atmosphere and determining, somewhere in the depths of instinct, whether the social climate offers to make the spirit bloom. I do not mean to say that a boy is as sensitive and accurate that way as a puppy is, but there is enough similarity between a very talented boy and a very dull puppy to mention it.

That Indian Maid was quite a dog. No one had

to tell you about her, once you saw her. She carried John Proctor's lemon ticking that you saw so much out of the famous nick with Lady Ferris, and she sort of reminded you of a violin string. She wasn't really nervous or shaky, but she was tuned real tight, and you could feel the tension humming in the air around her when she walked.

That is not always a good sign, because some promising young dogs that have it are unable to bear the strain they were born with and break under it and are not good for much of anything afterward. But when they do not break and are able to keep the tension and use it in their work, then it is a wonderful thing to see.

Uncle Ovid was very expert in helping young dogs keep it. He told me solemnly that he would have to admit he was very good at training dogs but that he was even better at not training them. For a long while I thought he was spoofing me, until I discovered that the very best trainers get that way by helping their dogs discover what they were born knowing, instead of trying to teach them everything.

There is enough to teach even the most talented

59

pups, anyway—the mechanical things, like ranging a course to cover it thoroughly in patterns and being staunch in the face of provocation and remaining steady to wing and shot when the excitement becomes almost unbearable even for people; and the purely mannered things, like honoring another dog's point. It is kind of like when a child is a musical prodigy—he still has to learn to read music and memorize passages and tune a violin, and it is all worthwhile because what he had when he started out is more than anyone could teach him.

Uncle Ovid dealt only in prodigies, he said. It was much easier to breed genius into a dog than to teach skill, he said. Grandsir said either it was much easier or else it was impossible, depending on the luck you had.

Indian Maid was the first example I saw, and she was a pretty good argument for Uncle Ovid's side. She had learned her yard manners, and she had been around Uncle Ovid while she was growing up, until she knew when he talked to her and a good deal of what he talked about. In the field, he let her run wild for a year, and that's the way she ran.

There is something in class dogs that makes them know they were put on earth to find birds, more birds than the next dog, and the only way for them to find more birds is to get out ahead, before any other dog gets there. They know it before they know anything else much, and sometimes before they find out, they run right out of the county.

When she began finding the birds while she was running, she had come to the critical stage where all her quality was at stake. The pointing instinct lies three hundred years deep in a bird dog, but it is a mysterious and incommunicable thing that may burst like a great light around a dog the first time he scents the hot, heady reek of game, or it may illuminate him very slowly and painfully and gradually over two or three years of his life. After that is when you teach him the rest, the intricate and perhaps arbitrary code of behavior expected of Open-All-Age dogs in field trial competition.

Maid was not entirely reconciled to the restrictions of manners in her derby year, although she ran regularly in the ribbons. It was not exactly that she lacked finish, I heard Grandsir say, so much as it was a kind of wild and desperate haste about her.

It has been a long time now, and perhaps they did not say that until afterward; then it would have been natural to see the desperation in the way she ran.

That was because there was a day when the ground was warm but the wind went east and blew freezing cold, and none of the dogs could find birds. Indian Maid was so frantic she went completely off the course, beyond sight of the boys riding out at the boundaries to keep track of the dogs, and all the way out of judgment. That wouldn't have been so bad. Frequently the fire burns up out of control in a fiery derby dog. But when they found her, she was caught in barbed wire and had cut the tendons across her right stifle to the bone.

On the way home, I asked Grandsir whether she would be all right, and he said, "No, boy, not really. She wanted to be a great dog, and, although she will get around all right, she will never run in the trials again, and that will be very hard on her."

For a while I did not say anything, feeling sorry for Indian Maid. Then I asked, "Why does any dog want to become a great dog?"

"I don't know," Grandsir said, "except that some of them can't help themselves."

And before I could ask the next question, he said, "That's the same reason that some men have for wanting to own them."

4

WHEN YOU HAVE SPENT all your life doing something, I guess you can't very well stop, at least not as long as there is anything left. Even after she was hurt, Indian Maid was quite a lot to have left. In the spring she went to the Commanche dog, and a number of people were real interested in the puppies that would come of that. I was not the most important person interested in that litter, but I tried hard to be the most conspicuous.

Uncle Ovid was looking forward to it, too.

"We'll be all right," he said. "We will raise us up a champion a couple of times over, once for his mother's wanting it and once for himself."

"Make it a triple champion," Grandsir said, "counting once for you, too. You can add one for the boy, too."

He seemed a little upset.

"Always the next one, Ovid," he said. "What happens when there is no next one?"

"I don't know," Uncle Ovid said seriously. "Cross that bridge when I get to it."

The Maid's puppies had arrived when we stopped in that summer at Thunder Hill. When we went out to the kennel, she came to the wire with that pleased wiggle some pointers have when they are truly pleased and not just being polite.

Grandsir looked at her and looked at me and folded his hands behind him under his coattails. Then he cleared his throat and spoke in the voice he used when he instructed a jury.

"Ovid," he announced gravely, "the boy thinks he wants a dog."

Uncle Ovid appeared quite taken aback. He pulled his head back and drew a fine sight on me with a squinted eye, shook his head, brushed his side-whiskers uphill thoughtfully, and finished by taking out his pipe and devoting several minutes to examining it.

"Well, well," he said, when it seemed I couldn't hold my breath any longer. "Think of that."

He and Grandsir stood there looking solemn and both thinking about it until I thought I was going to die right there. Apparently neither of them had much of a conclusion in sight, because after about five minutes, Uncle Ovid said, "Well, well."

Then he lighted his pipe very carefully. After that he announced it was time for supper, and we walked back up to the big house. I did not say very much, but I spoke when I was spoken to, and I devoted a good deal of attention to minding my manners. That was one thing Uncle Ovid and Grandsir seemed to agree on—how a boy should learn to mind his manners.

After supper we went out and sat on the porch. It was low-water time in the river, and the sound of the current splashing down exposed steps in the riverbed came gurgling up the hill, along with the smells of the marsh in bloom, like big breaking bubbles from the bottom of a pool. The dark was coming toward us from the far hills, and you could barely see the river. Uncle Ovid and Grandsir talked politics and the other things people talk about when they don't want to discuss anything really important, and I sat there on the steps being quiet.

Presently Uncle Ovid said, without any warning, "So you think you want a pup."

"Yes, sir," I said promptly.

"Well, well," mused Uncle Ovid, and I felt despair creeping up around me. But he didn't let it go this time.

"Mighty serious thing, boy," he said.

I said politely, "Yes, sir."

"What kind of a pup, boy?"

I understood him. He meant whether I preferred a pup out of a certain exclusive strain of English pointer, of any particular inclination—bold or aloof or eager or what. In those days you did not know, sometimes until you were a man grown, that there was any kind of dog except a pointing dog, and even after you found it out, it was sort of superfluous information, like knowing the Greek alphabet. So the way he put the question, I knew it was a kind of test, and I sat there thinking very hard.

It was a moment I did not forget afterward: the prairie sinking into darkness and twilight making the lawn immense and strange and the smell of Uncle Ovid's pipe a definite part of the moment.

I sorted out in my mind various replies and

determined to sound considered and mature, but it didn't sound exactly like that when I said, "The kind you remember after you grow up."

Grandsir made an approving sound from his side of the porch, and I thought it must be the lawyer in him approving an answer that didn't really answer any particular question, because he very seldom approved of anything anyone said about dogs.

Uncle Ovid was sitting in the rocking chair, and I could hear the boards give a little as he rocked himself. Grandsir murmured, "What are you smoking, Ovid?"

"Bright leaf," Uncle Ovid replied contentedly. "A little Burley. And a mite of St. James Parish rolled in."

Grandsir said, "Smells all right."

"Yup," said Uncle Ovid. "Tastes real nice."

I sat there and felt the chills run up and down my back. You never knew how these things were going to come out.

Presently Uncle Ovid said, "Your grandfather could tell you some things about picking that kind of a puppy, if he had a mind to."

"No," Grandsir said. "I am through with picking

puppies, Ovid. I am through with all of it, starting there."

"I reckon so," Uncle Ovid said. "Just wondered whether you might stretch a point for the boy." He said to me, "Reckon you can give me a definition of conformation?"

"Yes, sir," I said promptly. "Two of them. One is that conformation is what you have a right to talk about after you have studied twenty years or so and know the measurements of a thousand dogs of the blood across ten generations."

"Well," Uncle Ovid said. "What's the other?"

"That conformation is what you talk about at parties where some of the people haven't read the poems of Amy Lowell."

Grandsir coughed suddenly. Uncle Ovid said, "I see your grandmother still mentions dogs, off and on."

"Yes, sir," I said. "Sometimes."

Uncle Ovid tapped the dottle out of his pipe.

"We'll ponder on it some, tomorrow," he said.

I recognized the signal and went to bed while I was in good standing. It looked as though I had pleased both Grandsir and Uncle Ovid, somehow, and usually they were pleased by the opposite kinds of things.

Before breakfast in the morning, I went down to the kennel to see Indian Maid again and maybe catch a glimpse of the puppies. There were eight of them, but no one was allowed to get very close to them yet. Mr. Washington allowed me to go as far as the room where he mixed feed and stored tackle. From there I could peer into the gloom of Indian Maid's pen at the indefinite mass of squirming legs and bellies for about thirty seconds. Then Mr. Washington hustled me out.

At the table, I talked a good deal about Indian Maid and presently realized that another conversation was going on around me. Grandsir and Uncle Ovid were discussing with Mr. Washington's wife whether they should openly refer to the Maid as a bitch, on account of my being there, and Uncle Ovid said, "I declare, if a man just knew something about dogs, he might fuss about that word, and if he just knew something about ladies, he might. But if a man knows something about ladies and dogs both, I declare—"

Grandsir said violently, "Ovid!"

"Well, maybe you're right," Uncle Ovid said. "I'm a bachelor, myself."

From there, I thought we would go down to look at the puppies, but it turned out we were going hunting. That is, Grandsir and Uncle Ovid went hunting, and Mr. Washington and I rode in the buggy, once the dogs were cast off. I hoped they would take Indian Maid out for a little, but she was still nursing pups, and if you want to exercise a nursing bitch, you do it on the road, with horses, where there isn't any stubble to scratch her. That is the way you condition young dogs, too, when you don't want them to bump into birds and start thinking for themselves before you have a chance to help them think.

But we had a couple of the other dogs, and I wanted to discuss them, but Mr. Washington was busy watching. When the dogs did something pretty good, Mr. Washington said, "Oh, lordy, ain't that purely beautiful?" and I said, "Yes, sir."

After about an hour I realized that he didn't know I was there. So the next time the dogs did something and he said it, I said, "The backing dog wanted to break."

"What?" cried Mr. Washington indignantly. "Eh? Where you come from, boy?"

After that he knew I was there, and when nothing was going on, he would tell me about the old days when he first began to take care of the dogs at Thunder Hill. He was not very critical, but he had been there, and I liked to hear him tell about the times away back, like when the Gladstone heir by Noble won the first National, and the other two black dogs—black, white, and tan they were, he said, but all the folks called them black—by old Antonio won the next two and then no more except Monora.

Or even farther back, to the natives that either he remembered or someone had told him about so long ago it was like remembering—the Gildersleeves and the Morfords that were white and orange, and the Ethan Allens and the Sherwoods, and of course the Campbells that were bred to Elcho, who he said was the greatest Irish setter of all time and then some, and how the Campbells would have run the English setters into oblivion with their wonderful black crossbreds if it had not been for the individual power and glory of Gladstone.

73

Mr. Washington said the English setter people had started a rumor as how only sinful folks could breed black setters like the Campbells, but he allowed he had raised a black pup or two himself on the side and seemed sort of proud of it. I wondered how in the world I could comment on that and still be polite, but I didn't have to, because just then Uncle Ovid walked ahead of the horses with the gun Lou Smith's daddy made for him, all engraved and jeweled and inlaid with gold and silver and ivory, and shot three birds out of a covey with two shots, and all the rest of the afternoon Mr. Washington relapsed into saying, "Oh, lordy, that was purely beautiful," and that time he was right.

No one had to tell me about the way Uncle Ovid and Grandsir shot. They did it very formally, walking in on the dogs tall and straight, as though they were walking into a ballroom, perhaps stopping a moment to speak to the dog that had the find, then moving on into the birds, calmly and steadily, and when the covey burst, picking their birds and swinging on them with the easy, fluid grace that no man seems to develop unless he develops it killing something.

An artist with a gun is a basic artist, dealing in the medium of life and death. He makes a picture for you that you understand with a wrench in your bowels and sweat on your hands, because, without any tutoring at all, you realize that he has been willing to take up his responsibility over the life and the death and to make an art of it and to preserve and refine the art during the time when he does not need the killing. Some of the best artists with weapons are like Grandsir, who very rarely killed a full bag of birds, but once in a while he would kill one quickly and cleanly and beautifully, so that you did not forget he had done it and could do it whenever it was necessary.

It was easy for me to see why my daddy had disappointed Grandsir with his shooting, because he was so impatient to get on with the killing, no one found out whether he had any real talent for it or just a superficial aptness. But for myself, after watching Uncle Ovid and Grandsir shoot that year, I made up my mind I would study very hard. And while I did study, and practiced diligently for a long time, I finally became reconciled to a certain highly specialized branch of the art which consists of making very easy shots look very difficult, if not impossible.

One thing about the dogs Mr. Washington couldn't answer for me. I had seen them running in the trials before I saw them really hunting, and it seemed to me that the best of the trial dogs loved the birds so much that they couldn't bear it if, instead of a handler shooting a blank pistol to signify the shot, the birds should really be killed. I put the question to Grandsir, and he surprised me by taking quite a while to explain.

"Death is the reality, boy," he said gravely. "We all have to face it. The men and the dogs and the birds. That is what we have in common, the living and then the dying, and the dying is an important part of the living. No one has a right to ignore that, and everyone has a responsibility to recognize it. But you are right, boy," he said, "about how the best dogs love the birds. The love is what weaves together the living and the dying and makes it complete, and the greater the love is in the living, the more beautiful and memorable should be the dying."

Somehow I had a feeling he was not talking about birds alone, but I didn't know what to say, and then

Uncle Ovid started the talk back to dogs again by telling how the difference between a fine trial dog and a shooting dog was like the difference between a butcher and a surgeon cutting up a hog. The butcher does it well, Uncle Ovid said, because it is his work and all he knows, but the doctor does it casually, as a favor to his wife maybe, but does it cleaner and better, and it does not take a fraction of his skill or talent or knowledge.

"Like that time," Uncle Ovid said, "when Mr. Duryea and Mr. Lorillard argued about the two kinds, and Jim Avent put down the trialers against Mr. Lorillard's shooting dogs."

He shook his head sadly.

"It was real pitiful. Even without Sioux it would have been bad, but Jim Avent put down the greatest setter who ever lived, and when she did to the shooting dogs what she couldn't help doing, it was real pitiful."

It started to drizzle about suppertime that night and was too damp to sit on the porch. There was a fire in the fireplace, though, and I got an apple and pushed it over in a corner where I could heap hot ashes on it to keep busy. I did not want to go to bed, and if I didn't keep busy, I would go to sleep and fall right in with the bur oak rounds.

There were good pictures here at Thunder Hill, too. The familiar one of Rip Rap was there, the one that shows him with a tail like an otter and a topline like an Arkansas hog, and also the one that every dog man ought to hang over his desk, so that when he becomes unduly proud of handsome conformation, he can look up at the very foundation and pillar of the pointer in America and stay humble.

There was the wonderful picture of Becky Broomhill, who then was very young and just coming on, but there was no doubt of her, and a very bad picture of Commanche Frank, where Lady John's son is represented as pointing something, and from the expression on his face, it was an outhouse, because he was not famous for his nose, but he sure smelled something. There were pictures of Ripple and Jingo and John Proctor and Manitoba Rap and the Whitestone and Gladstone and Mohawk setters and smaller pictures like the ones at home, of High Valor and Stanford Lad and the rest.

I was sitting there, watching my apple, my eyebrows a little singed from not quite staying awake for a second, when Grandsir and Uncle Ovid came in and sat down in the chairs on each side of me.

Presently Uncle Ovid cleared his throat as a warning and said, "I reckon you'll be getting along home one of these days."

"It's time," Grandsir said. "You ready, boy?"

"Well," I said indefinitely.

"Pshaw, we got to cut this bedevilin' out," Uncle Ovid said. "Boy, it appears to me we better go down see the Maid in the morning and let you pick out a puppy."

"Me?" I finally squeezed out in a small, painful voice.

"Why, I do believe it's you," Uncle Ovid said jocularly. "I don't believe I see any other young 'uns mooning around here making up to mother dogs and such like."

"Yes, sir," I said. "No, sir. But I didn't know I was going to get to pick one myself."

"Yup," Uncle Ovid said. "I calculate a man's entitled to make his own mistakes."

The sentence had an uncommon familiarity, like maybe it was an old family motto. I sat there paralyzed for quite a while.

"Grandsir—" I got out finally.

"Don't bother to ask, boy," Grandsir said. "No one can help you, and maybe you can't help yourself. You don't have free will in selecting a personal dog any more than you will have in selecting a wife. You are conditioned to a pattern by your life before you are old enough to know it, and you have to choose what fits your pattern. Some men cannot pick a bad wife or a good dog, and vice versa. That is why I do not pick pups for anyone."

Uncle Ovid started to say something, and Grandsir said impatiently, "Don't be ridiculous, Ovid. It is that I cannot pick a bad dog, either, even now, and some people could not forgive me for that."

I hunched my stool even closer to the fire and heaped coals on my apple. By the time I remembered what I was doing, you couldn't tell the apple from the cinders.

Anyway, the next morning we went down to the kennels, Uncle Ovid looking pleased and Grandsir looking not pleased and me walking between, feeling mostly numb.

Uncle Ovid unlocked the kennel door and we went into the feedroom, and Uncle Ovid brought the eight puppies out where we could look them over. Seven of them were as pretty as any pointers you ever saw, white and lemon and slick-looking even at that age. The eighth one, though—there was something else. He was big, for one thing; you're supposed to shy away from the biggest pup in the litter. And he was ugly—my goodness, yes. His head was solid liver, and you could tell from the first time you saw him he was going to have a predatory Roman nose; it couldn't possibly straighten out enough as his muzzle developed. To go with it, he had a flat skull and ears too high, with thick leathers. When his eyes came open, they were light, not as blue as usual, and you knew he was going to have a strange pale stare instead of the warm brown.

I was such a kid, and scared, and every time I looked at that dog with the liver head, I had a queasy feeling in my stomach. When I put my hand down, the other seven tumbled over and licked it violently, then grabbed my fingers in their little needle teeth and growled. The liver-headed dog did not bother to look. I put my hand over beside him, and he

81

looked away. I took hold of his head and turned it, and he opened his eyes and looked at me. I wish he hadn't; I never stopped wishing he hadn't, afterward—the baby eyes, but cloudy and strange, strange, strange.

"Well," Uncle Ovid said, "which one?"

There was that awful, sick feeling that made my knees feel weak, and I looked at Grandsir, but he was watching a spider walk around on the ceiling. I took a deep breath and knew when I said it that this was the beginning of something, but the white dog with the dark head had looked me full in the eye, and I couldn't help it.

"That's the one," I said.

Algonquin.

Uncle Ovid's weathered face, so warm and fine behind the white whiskers, lighted up with his beaming smile, and he clapped me on the shoulder and said fine, but Grandsir did not say anything at all. I wondered whether it was because I picked as he would have picked or the other way, but he didn't tell me. It was just as well I thought about that, instead of maybe thinking how no one could make a better choice, nor a worse one, from that litter, and how maybe no one ever would see Uncle Ovid smile that way again.

"We'll have another look later on," Grandsir said. "Next month, when we come back for the chicken shooting."

But we didn't. The fire fixed that.

II

After the fire, I tried to tell Grandsir something about Indian Maid and Algonquin and the way I felt, but it didn't come out right, and he said, "Never mind, boy, I understand." Maybe he did, but I didn't; it was like knowing an important secret that was in a foreign phrase you had memorized but couldn't translate until you learned a whole new language.

5

FOR A WHILE after I was home again, the details of the fire at Thunder Hill were very close to the surface of my memory, but, like someone trying to walk very carefully on skim ice, I tried not to look down and see them. Still, I would wake at night, whimpering about the red glare in my bedroom, or I would hear the dogs scream in my dreams and wake up shouting something, but I never knew what it was I said. It seemed important that I should.

One time I almost had it. I was sitting up in bed, and I could still hear the echoes of my voice, and by straining my ears I could hear the bouncing fragments of the syllables, but just then Grandma came into the room to see what the noise was about and put her hand on my head and pushed me back down on the pillow.

"Wait a minute, please," I cried. "I just heard what I said; please, just a minute, let me listen."

"All right, sir, you listen." Grandma was a vast and indistinct bulk in the room, but her voice was bold and full, as usual.

"What did I say?" For some reason, I began to cry.

Grandma's voice said, "Why do you want to know, boy?"

"Because." That was boy's logic. Because I'd know something then, something terribly important about dogs or about people or about fires or about dying. I grabbed her hand in the gloom. "Do you know what I said?"

She pushed me back on the pillow and rubbed my forehead a moment before taking her hand away.

"You said, 'Tomorrow is Tuesday,' " she said.

For a moment I was silent. Then I said, "That doesn't sound like a riddle or anything."

Why did it have to be a riddle?

"Surely it does, boy." I could feel Grandma's bulk tremble with laughter. "It verges on prophecy."

The only trouble was, tomorrow was Friday.

So that was that. I never remembered or understood, not then or now. In a little while, though, it did not matter, because the details of the real fire became so lurid and extensive in my recollection that presently I realized they were not the real details at all but instead were things I had imagined afterward. Then, when I no longer was able to distinguish between the real and imagined memory, I was safe.

I told Grandma that, and she said that there appeared to be a possibility I would understand some of the things Grandsir said, after all, if I kept it up.

Grandma was very helpful usually. She was a great big, delicate-looking woman, sort of like a white stone church, if you know what I mean. She always wore black velvet and carried a cane with a silver head, mostly for tapping on the floor when she wanted to emphasize a point, and around her throat she wore a black ribbon with things in it that sparkled when she sparkled and glittered coldly when she was angry. They turned out to be diamonds, but that didn't mean anything to me at the time.

She had white, wavy hair and a hawk-browed,

amused face that made me dissatisfied with the appearance of grandmotherly-type women forever afterward. Few enough women can convince you they are beautiful when they are young and all the things that help them pass for beautiful are fresh. When they grow old, they mostly give up trying to convince anyone they still are beautiful, because there is no point in it, and instead they tell you how beautiful they were when they were young, which they weren't, but it does not hurt anything, except it makes you think how a woman's youth is like a plug shooting dog: The longer ago and farther away it was, the more the owner warms to telling you how splendid it was.

But Grandma was beautiful in a way not many women are. You could see that in the picture of her that hung in the hall, where everyone coming into the house saw it. It was painted when she was a girl, and I knew when I was very young that she was beautiful in it, because I heard her say so. I heard her one Christmas Eve when the senator was there, and her other brother, who was a commodore and who embittered me against the naval forces earlier that night because he did not wear his magnificent uniform.

Anyway, they were there, and the ladies and all, and Grandma stopped in front of the picture and rapped her cane smartly on the floor and said, "By Godfrey, gentlemen, I was a lovely wench."

And afterward she laughed, her full-throated, hearty laughter, and she could do that because she had not lost any of the beauty, and all the other ladies hated her, even the young ones, but they were afraid of her, too, and I guess that's how Grandma liked to have it.

As I said, she was very good with me. She did not ask a lot of questions, and, for that matter, looking back, I can see she did not answer many of them, either, but whenever I was lonesome or blue or wanted someone to talk to, she was there, and just talking to her made everything smooth out and be all right.

For a long time after we came home from the fire, I did not want to talk about dogs. Gradually, though, the shock wore off. When my confidence in the authenticity of details was shaken, the nightmare quality became merely dreamlike, and it seemed sort of vague and unlikely, as though it were a graphic story someone had told me that I remembered for a while but that faded, the way stories will.

When I got to that point, I began thinking of the pup again and daydreaming about him and what a fine dog he would be and, perhaps looming even larger in the daydreams, how fine I would look and with what merit. Oh, I would cut a dashing figure; I would cultivate a casual grace and a gallant modesty, and, like Uncle Ovid, I would grow side-whiskers (white) and be a heck of a fellow, even though I would not chew tobacco. I already tried that once and did not plan to repeat the deplorable experiment.

But I had my dog handling career all visualized. When a boy loses touch with reality, the hands of his imagination are freed, and once the circulation gets back into them, they really can turn out some productions in fantasy.

In keeping with my projected career in field and drawing room, I outlined to myself the steps by which I would impart to Algonquin the surpassing skill that would make him a derby champion and me the boy wonder of the big circuit. I labored in spirit, conditioning him on the gravel roads to toughen his feet, roading him miles on the long leash, and teaching him to course wide by pushing at him with a galloping horse. Because his mother had been a trifle wild, I foresaw how I would have trouble steadying him and how I would cleverly overcome the wildness with a check cord, long enough at first to hold him but then gradually shortened until only the snap remained but was enough to remind him. Then I would teach him high style to go with his staunchness, and this by a training process so mysterious that I couldn't even figure it out into a reasonable dream, because I knew as well as anyone that style is a part of quality, and the quality of a dog is something like the tail of a dog: Either he has it or he hasn't.

At this point, it seemed obvious that my imagined triumphs in the trials should follow in order, but I was stymied. These concocted victories naturally needed to be spectacular, indeed overwhelming, and my imagination failed me, with its products turning pale by comparison with the mighty facts embodied in the gold cups and silver plates and faded rosettes all around me and with the fabulous histories Grandma knew.

More often, now, I would corner her in the library, and she would make a conscientious gesture of evading me, but if I were very determined, she would give in presently and sink into one of the old leather chairs, sitting slowly at first, then faster, like a tree falling, until she was down. Then she would heave a long sigh and fold her lovely hands on the silver head of the cane. She would wheeze a little getting her breath and look at me with an eyebrow cocked rakishly and wink, maybe.

"Well, sir?"

Perhaps it would be one of the almost legendary chronicles she told, one she had heard from her own father, of the Campbell strain, those crossbred Gordon-Irish-English wonder dogs that came out of Tennessee to make miracles; of Mason's Jeff and Old Fan, who never produced a pup that fell short of nobility; of Night, who won the first Free-for-All; and of Joe, Jr., greatest of all the Campbells, who ran the immortal Gladstone into the ground during an astounding two-day endurance test, where nothing counted but birds pointed.

Or she might move on well into her own time and recount the National Championship of 1909, when

Alford's John, who was maybe the smartest bird dog who ever lived, went down in his ninth year and had his most lasting fame won in defeat, for he drew Manitoba Rap, running the climactic race of his career. From there, she might drift backward a year to when Fishel's Frank was called the uncrowned champion after he ran in a brace with Danfield, even though Danfield and another setter, Count Whitestone II, were called back, and Danfield won. The judges put down Mr. Fishel's dog, she said, because he took a rude step forward in the presence of game.

Or, again, she might talk of our own dogs, of High Valor or Stanford Lad or Riptide or Prime Minister or Roanoke or First Lord. Those were the times I liked best, because she would forget a little that she was talking to me and would talk to herself; her vibrant and melodious voice would conjure up the memorable past then in a kind of magic. Sitting there in the big dark room, I would feel myself beneath a sun that blazed down on the prairie stubble of Saskatchewan of an afternoon many years before. Or I would thrill to the pound of racing feet across hard Georgia clay as two champions were cast off together. Under that spell, the old, old air of dust and unopened books would fade, and I could smell the crushed pine needles from one end of the big circuit mingling with the pungence of sedge and the heady reek of clover from the other.

In the talking, sometimes she forgot all about me and did not mention the dogs but instead remembered people and places. I heard of the glittering balls at Thunder Hill to announce a litter and of the ladies and gentlemen in formal dress at the banquets on the night of a draw. That was where the owners did their own drawing to see what dogs would be braced together in the heats. The pattern of it soaked into me almost without my knowing: the democracy of quality, where the man who ran the drugstore and the general's son were friends and competitors, and the men who handled bird dogs were gentlemen. There was dreadful snobbery there, too, but it was not meant that way, because the arrogance was part of the quality, too. That was the measure in everything—pure quality in people and dogs and manners. You never said a proud thing of your own dogs or a harsh thing about anyone else's, but sometimes you were allowed to smile.

I do not mention this because it was so fine or desirable but because it was a system that came and grew and flourished and then passed away. It was all tied up with the dogs that were so important to a certain way of life for some reason no one ever put into words, because words might spoil it. The way of life was hard and demanding and in a way brutal, but still it built a code of grace and charm and beauty for those who believed in it, a way of life that never could have been, except for the dogs. Grandma said that when you were part of that life, you had to be uncompromising enough to admit that, to some people, the dogs really were more important than most other people. The way of life had faded away quite completely in my time, but I never stopped to wonder whether it was because more dogs became less important or fewer people became more important—or what.

Grandsir came in during one such time, when she had talked the color high in her cheeks and her voice was tight and happy with a stirring history. First he looked a little angry, but the stern look faded presently, and he seemed only puzzled.

"What a strange thing, madam," he said. "You

do not say anything about the loss and waste and grief."

"Why"—Grandma seemed surprised, too—"it is a strange thing, sir. And you will recall," she said, "that I was very bitter."

At that, she laughed musically, as though someone had said something funny, but no one else had said anything. Then she rapped her cane and wheeled around in her chair like she was a gun turret being pivoted to point at me.

"You, sir," she said smartly, making me feel as though I had just walked into the room and done something uncouth. "You, sir, get about your business, sir."

"Yes, ma'am." I left hastily.

But there was a funny thing about going outside from the library after talking to Grandma. Outside, it always seemed to be less bright, less sunny, less exciting, somehow, than it had been in the dark old room where you could make magic with words.

What Grandsir had said worried me, though, and afterward I mentioned that she never had said anything about those other things, and he nodded gravely and looked off somewhere else.

I said, "Maybe that is something else I have a right to learn for myself."

Right away I could tell I shouldn't have said that, although I was just reviewing prospects. Grandsir winced and put his arm around me quickly and quickly took it away, and for just a moment, the only time I ever knew, he was not quite sure what to do.

Seeing him like that, I was very embarrassed and started to apologize, but it did not come out right and I wound up blubbering, and Grandsir very thankfully got angry and declared, "Great heavens, boy, be patient. You do not need to weep until you find out firsthand the nature of events that require it."

So it turned out all right that time, but I knew Grandsir remembered it. He came back to it finally, after the year had rolled around and we were on our way back to Thunder Hill. The time was long past, of course, when a shred of true recollection remained with me to threaten the record of the kennel fire as I imagined it, and I was very cheerful.

We were sitting side by side on the green plush cushions of the railroad car, and Grandsir said how he had been very selfish and I must forgive him.

That almost startled me back to normal.

"Why, sir?"

"Perhaps I have not been fair to you, boy. But I want you to understand it isn't because I intended to be unfair. It is that possibly I lost sight of what a boy thinks and what he needs." He paused and took a deep breath and added, "You must understand, boy, that if you have been treated badly in the matter of dogs, it is not because I care any less about you but because I do not care so much about dogs anymore."

"Yes, sir," I said. I was deeply moved, but still I noticed the technical precision of his phrasing; he said he did not care so much about dogs anymore, but that did not tell you how much he had cared or how much in proportion was left.

"All right, then," he said, relaxing. "Just so you know. Someday you will look back, as I do, and you will know that if you want the good times with the dogs, you must have the bad times, also, and that it is only through the bad times and the bad-acting, no-good, bad-hearted dogs that you earn the good times and perhaps one great dog, if you prove very faithful with the moderately good ones. And when it is all over," he said, "you can look back, as I have, and then you will have to decide for yourself whether the good times were worth the bad and whether the great dog, if you have him, was worth any of it."

I could not let go of it. I said, "But there is always the grief and the waste?"

"Yes," Grandsir said very quietly and very sadly and very firmly. "There is always the grief and the waste, and that is what you have to decide: whether you are strong enough for grief to risk having more than one great dog."

After that we did not talk anymore.

6

MR. WASHINGTON met us at the Junction, as usual. I was so happy to be back I did not notice, but all the way out he hardly said anything. Things were some different at Thunder Hill, too, but I didn't notice that, either. Uncle Ovid was standing at the top of the porch steps and started down as I started up, and the regular preliminaries were gone through, as usual. His moustache was a little untidy, maybe, and his suit might have been rumpled, but I did not pay any attention to that. All I could think about was the pup and what he would look like and all, so that I was in a fine sweat until Uncle Ovid shook hands with me and I told him fervently how purely glad I was to be there.

"You'd better go see your dog," he said then, and I bobbed politely and scampered down the walk

102

and around the house, and right there I had a terrible shock. Somehow it did not seem possible that the kennels were really gone. Of course, if I had stopped to think about it, I'd have known, but I hadn't stopped, and for some reason I thought the fire had been a dream, too, like my recollection of it, and I had fully expected, when I dashed around the summerhouse, to find everything as it had been.

I never thought of it that way again.

For a few minutes I stood there, scuffing one toe against the hard little stones of the walk, looking at the rusty, sagging wire draped over the framework of the old runs and the rectangle of foundation still full of raw black beams and debris. Right where Indian Maid's box had been you could see the edge of a battered dish, and I remembered once I had been allowed to mix a meal in it and put it down there, and no one would pick it up again, not ever.

The kennels were burned for me then. They were burned and gone, and the memory was gone, and it was like there never had been any kennels there but only the charred ruins of something I did not quite recollect.

After that, I turned and walked slowly back to the house, a little older again, all in a few minutes. That is the way the dogs age you. They age you very fast in very short periods, and in between they let you stay the same age, so that many of the people who have to do with dogs are either very young or very old, and the ones who age normally know how it is and sometimes feel a little discomfited, as though they do not fully belong to the brotherhood, and maybe they don't. I walked back to the house older, as I say, and wiser but not any happier for being wiser.

The kitchen door was nearest, so I opened it and started in, then backed right out again. There was a dog in there—my goodness, I should say so. He looked like no dog I ever saw before, all tight and on tiptoe, as though he might be touched off with a trigger, maybe, or a fuse, and if he were he would do things you never saw before, either.

Physically he was some machine, with the splendid symmetry of power, the pure force of bone and shoulders and chest and thighs, all fluidly molded together, but you never noticed those things, seeing him all at once, and I didn't, either, afterward, for

104

he walked toward the door and came into full light, and I saw his head. That made you forget the wonderfully effective machinery. His head was solid liver, the color of bitter chocolate, with a full Roman muzzle and flaring, marvelous nostrils like fabulous jewels lost out of their rightful settings, the blood vessels so dense and well developed and close to the surface you could almost count his pulse; you noticed that and the eyes, really yellow and so remote, so cold, maybe sardonic, but still strange, strange, strange.

I stared at him, fascinated, and he looked back at me, knowing me as I knew him.

Algonquin.

Uncle Ovid came into the kitchen behind me and saw me peering through the screen.

"So you found your dog," he said jovially. "How do you like him?"

I stammered something polite, but I was looking at the dog and he was looking back, and suddenly I wished that I had never started this, that I had never wanted a puppy and had never known Indian Maid and had never come to Thunder Hill, but it was no good wishing. I looked into those golden eyes, and we both knew it was no good; there was something between us, and we would have to use it up. There is no way to give in easily.

You see, frequently it is very difficult to acquire a dog, particularly if he is an important dog, but if he is truly important in some way, and you associate him with yourself over a period of time, acquiring him is nothing at all, in the way of difficulty, compared to the trouble you have trying to disassociate yourself from him. I was linked to that dog by some strange bond, emotional or superstitious or whatever you want to call it, but he was my dog before he was born, and I knew I was involved with him for whatever there was ahead of us, and he knew it, too. Maybe that is why he seemed amused, and surely it was why I felt enmeshed in something soft and clinging, as though I pushed myself into a net of spider webs.

Oh, he was quite a dog by then, even at that age. Later on, Grandsir watched him out on the lawn, running with that easy, effortless motion that made you think of unrelated comparisons—as much like a locomotive as like thistledown. Grandsir looked serious, and that moment was the beginning of a long, long time during which Grandsir looked progressively more serious.

"Who does he move like?" Uncle Ovid's question sounded like one of those you get in a test, where there is only one answer.

"You have to go back a long way," Grandsir said. "It is a long time to remember."

"You could never forget," Uncle Ovid said triumphantly. "No one who saw Drake's gait could ever forget."

I suppose Grandsir and Uncle Ovid were two of the last people who could talk about seeing Sir Richard Garth's Drake, from when they were boys my age and went to England with their daddy when the general was buying dogs. Grandsir told me that in the beginning there were Bounce and Hamlet and Major and Drake, like archangels of the English pointer. Then, he said, Sam Price—not the Honorable Lloyd—brought out Bang, and it was like when the Lord created Adam. I said that was a good way to remember, and Grandsir said, "Oh, yes, indeed, reading the Good Book is very fruitful."

The reason Algonquin made them mention Drake must have been that Drake was so blazing fast that they say of him it was not until he had run through seven seasons that time brought his speed down to the rate where he could make a normal standing point without skidding.

"He does not have so much claim on Drake," Grandsir said thoughtfully. "Mostly his stock goes back through Rip Rap and King of Kent and Priam to Price's Bang."

"Who was straight out of Whitehouse's Hamlet and Brockton's Bounce," I said brashly, but no one paid any attention. I knew the fourth one of the cornerstones, too: Statter's Major.

"Spare me the charts," Uncle Ovid said to Grandsir, not angry but with a certain tone in his voice. "Spare me the mathematics of prepotency."

That is the way a stud dog is bred to insure that he passes on certain things to his offspring, regardless of their various mothers; it is the power he has of reproducing himself.

"As precise as differential calculus," Grandsir said, talking about the science of breeding. "As valuable to posterity as the rules of torts and contracts, and as unshakable as the form of Latin grammar."

"Oh, I believe you." Uncle Ovid's voice still had the tone; I recognized it finally—exhilarated. "I believe you intellectual fellows have it all figured out. Only sometimes, when you ain't looking, God fixes up a surprise for you."

Grandsir said, "I will not contest it with you. He moves very well, and it is not like a puppy."

"He moves like the wrath of God," Uncle Ovid said exultantly. "And he never had no puppyhood."

That seemed a funny thing to me, but I guess it was true. Maybe it was because he didn't have time, maybe because he was all alone. Whatever it was, Algonquin skipped over that period of endearing gracelessness.

Uncle Ovid said, "He was born old, and one of the things made him ugly was having to wait so long for his body to grow up to his wits." He paused and peered at us with a happy, secret expression. "But it's catching up. You'll see."

We did, too. Mr. Washington had a dog Uncle Ovid let him keep down in the stable because Mr. Washington said the poltergeists would get the horses or something without a stable dog, and we took her. She was an uncertain little whippet

of a setter who did not know very much about birds
and cared less, but she could run, all right, although
that morning you would not have believed it, the
way Algonquin ran away from her. He did not
make any particular point of it; he just acted as
though it was too bad, but, of course, he couldn't
wait, and he ran away from her so effortlessly that
presently she became enraged and went home, and
Mr. Washington had to go after her.

Grandsir and Uncle Ovid and I watched Algonquin for a while, and I do not have any idea how
Drake ran, except for what Uncle Ovid said, but if
that was the way, it was no wonder what they said
about him. It is possible that many have been that
fast and that some have been as casual about it, but
you'll never convince me. It was no more work for
him than it was for lightning that just flickers across
the horizon. I knew there was a question in Grandsir's mind, and so did Uncle Ovid, because he
arranged the dog's course so that his answer beat
Grandsir's question.

We came to a barrier of vegetation that had been
allowed to grow wild, as a shelterbelt and cover
avenue where the birds could move without fear of

predators among the thorn apple trees and raspberries and, worse yet, blackberries, and over it a dense netting of grapevines. There was just a tiny change in Algonquin's gait, a brightening almost, as though he recognized a challenge and welcomed it, and he hit the barrier, and you stood there with your mouth open while the dust and the leaves and the dead twigs settled down over the path he made through it like a fast freight going through a stalled buggy.

Grandsir went back and mounted his horse and arranged the reins very carefully in his hand.

"Let us go down into the preserve," he said, "and see if the chickens are lying in as yet."

Now, in those days, there was a yardstick by which you could measure the merit of a bird dog in precise fractions, and the yardstick was called the prairie chicken.

There was something about chickens that, if you knew them well, nothing else really mattered. You were very polite when other men talked about the little brown gentleman called bobwhite, and you nodded courteously to hear the praises of the ruffed grouse, but you had your own knowledge safe and sure in your heart. I was just old enough in those

112

days to recognize that old Yellow Legs stood for a whole era and barely old enough to know what I was going to miss.

Grandsir was very careful that I did not find out too much about chickens, because he said that if I established any kind of personal relationship with them, I would not be satisfied with lesser birds afterward, and he said one dissatisfied man in the family was enough. He would be a great plenty, all by himself, he said wryly. I thought he was fooling then, but he wasn't.

At the time, I didn't understand why there wouldn't be any more prairie chickens by and by, and when I asked Grandsir, he said that, because they were very faithful to ecological patterns, they would continue to follow the bison, and the bison already were well on their way to Limbo.

I never had heard of that place and asked him if we couldn't go there, and Grandsir said it was possible, indeed likely, that he would, but he didn't know about me, since the regulations were very strict. He did not understand, he said, why more people did not attempt to qualify for Limbo, because a great many fine people were there already. Limbo

113

was especially good for the hunting, he said, warming up to the subject as he went along; why, on birds alone, beside the chickens, there would be heath hens and spruce grouse and wild turkeys and the flocks of passenger pigeons sweeping up in clouds that could turn a sunny day to dusk.

I asked him why they had so many things there in Limbo that we didn't have anymore.

"It is very sad, in a way." Grandsir picked up his reins to follow the dog. "But it appears that they have gotten all the best game managers away from us, too."

Over on the side, Uncle Ovid had an expression to his eyebrows that seemed fairly definite, but, even so, I was pretty sure that Grandsir wasn't entirely fooling.

But that does not tell you about the chickens and Algonquin. The first time I saw him, the chickens were there for him. Chickens were different in several ways from the birds we have now. On grouse, for instance, a dog's difficulties come from the heavy cover and the iron-nerved way partridge can withhold scent. On pheasant, a dog is troubled because the wily Oriental is no gentleman about staying where you point him and on top of it can outrun a medium fast dog if he has any cover. The bobwhite is a very polished gentleman and very courteous, and that is what makes him the great field trial bird. His splendid manners present the highest possible standard of comparison for a dog's manners, and what you want there is the very purest kind of comparison.

The chickens, though, were not gentlemen as such; they were quite apart from what that word means. They were stern aristocrats, the no-compromise few who would rather die than accept even a little change in their system. They were very wise and very wild and, when flocked up, were in addition so beautifully organized as a feudal unit that they could make even a sophisticated dog look extremely foolish.

They did not have any compassion toward clumsy hunters as quail do, but on the other hand they did not stoop to any devious subterfuges like pheasant. They have left a family attitude much modified in their sharp-tailed kin, but you had to know them to understand their attitude. When it came to dogs, the chickens would deal only with a high, hard, fast master who came upon them like a storm and put the spell of his will over them like the shadow of doom and spoke to them compellingly, and if he was equal to this commission, then you had a thing of beauty to remember.

But if a dog was hesitant or unsure or even let the heat of his intensity diminish faintly, the sentries' heads would move contemptuously in the grass, and the chickens would get up like a line squall bursting on the prairie and would go away from you.

In our time there were two dogs that, if you saw either of them on chickens, would have provided you with a standard to go by. One of them was Hard Cash, who was by Lad of Jingo, a son of the great Jingo out of Dot's Pearl, a Rip Rap bitch. The other was Algonquin.

When we were through and came in that first day, Grandsir asked in a very earnest tone, "Ovid, what are you planning to do with that dog?"

"Why"—Uncle Ovid appeared very innocent—"I thought that I would smooth him up a mite and let the boy take him on home."

"Oh, to be sure," Grandsir said. "Let the boy take him home."

"Well," Uncle Ovid said, "he's the boy's dog, you know."

"That is exactly what I need," Grandsir said. "After all these years, a dog like that in my house. Just once again. Just one more dog like that in my house."

"Algonquin." Uncle Ovid used it like a kind of a talisman to hold up in front of him when Grandsir pressed too hard. The word that was a name: Algonquin.

No one ever talked to that dog or about him except by that word. He had no nickname, no call name, no endearments. He was like someone you have in your house and you don't know for sure who he is, but you have a word to call him by, and you use it for a name and think maybe after a while you will find out about him, but you never do.

"Algonquin."

This time, Grandsir said it.

"Algonquin." He said it again, and the veins swelled suddenly in his forehead and his face turned dark, and he stood up to his full height in his black judge's clothes, and his voice had the full, lashing courtroom tones, and I want to tell you I never heard a man talk the way he talked to Uncle Ovid.

"No, Ovid," he said. "You do not really plan to give the boy this dog. You plan to keep him if he kills you, and I think he may. Oh, yes, Ovid"— Grandsir's voice began sliding down the scale so it could get a rising start on the next sentence— "already you begin to cherish him, in your old age, with your small remaining time. You plan to pour out your bitterness on him in an orgy of waste, to squander the last tattered shreds of your resources, because you have grown from a wild young fool into a fierce old fool, and you could no more willingly part with this dog, who will destroy you, than you can fly."

We had put away the horses and walked into the house and were in the room with the wall of little panes, where you could look over the blended sections of prairie to the hills. Uncle Ovid rocked a little from the torrent of Grandsir's language, but he stayed standing by the windows, looking out.

"I know it." He sounded like I might have sounded, admitting I had done something wrong and planning to do it again.

"Once I could look out here and see the Old

Place stretching out from Thunder Hill as far as you can see, the way you and I did years ago, and the way our daddy could from the time he had the grant from the chiefs. And now it's going, all right, and I reckon I know as well as most how it shouldn't.'"

He looked at me as though I was affected, and maybe I was.

"'I'll sell it, piece by piece, while I get older and weaker and crazier, and I'll take this dog where he's got to go.'"

Grandsir was looking at him with a look that might have been anger or might have been sorrow or might even have been love.

Uncle Ovid said in a shaking voice, "If the boy don't take this dog, I'll do what I have to do because he's the last one, from any way you look at it, and when we're dead and gone, they'll say it: There never was a dog like Algonquin."

He did not turn around, and even I knew why. He was weeping, not the loose way an old man cries but the hard way, without tears.

"All right." Grandsir sounded dreadful, so quiet and hopeless. "You have seen it all before."

119

"Yes," Uncle Ovid said.

"You know how it is," Grandsir said. "The pups —always the best pups—that are taken off by distemper, and how the hookworm or the whipworm takes what the germs miss."

"Yes," Uncle Ovid said. "That's the easy way."

"Oh, I know it well," Grandsir said. "I know it is a true thing that the distemper or the strep or the encephalitis or hard pad saves you time and tears. But the will of God is not easy, not when it leaves Indian Maid caught in the wire—" he drew a deep breath, and suddenly in that great room a bell began to toll, for my grandfather was calling up the mighty dead—"or Stanford Lad coughing out his lifeblood with the fever, or Roanoke destroyed by a rabid beast within sight of the gallery"—those were the names, now, the great ones—"or Prime Minister lighted like a torch by a brush fire, or Riptide shot down by a drunken trespasser—" he hesitated, as though he would gag on his own words, for this was close, close to my grandfather's heart and long buried there—"or Blue Dan lying dead in the ditch beside a railroad in Tennessee, or High Valor"—that was the name of all the names—"Val, big Val, poisoned by my best friend because he could not bear that such a dog should live and not be his."

He called that awful roll, the mighty names and the terrible things that happened to them, all the shocking secrets I had never heard before, and then he said, as if he were very tired, "So you are assured now that none of these things will happen to Algonquin. Ovid, if you make your pact with the devil, remember that you must be strong when it comes time to pay."

I never saw my grandfather like that before, but I heard his voice once, echoing in the same tones, on one distant day in his courtroom when they hurried me away because they did not think I should hear him tell a man that he must die for something he had done.

7

AFTER HEARING GRANDSIR toll off his dogs and how they died, I did not sleep very well. When you are young, it seems that all the great events that came before your time were fashioned of immortal stuff and acted out by gods and demigods. The great dogs you never knew are like the great men in history books, whose names and deeds you learn so young that their position in the past is fixed as firmly as Polaris in his place—as clean and distant and incommunicable, too.

Later, when they tell you, for instance, that General Washington looked so stern and worried because he had false teeth and they hurt his mouth, you are disillusioned for a little while. But presently you find it was so, and some other things as well, but General Washington was no less himself without his teeth than with them, and you accept this demeaning, or at least mortalizing, condition and grow a little older, wiser, and sadder. Sometimes it seemed to me that a boy had nothing else to face but gloomy prospects of growing always older, always wiser, always sadder.

That was how I felt the night Grandsir talked about his dogs. Even then I had reached the point where I was very jealous of a few remaining illusions. And somehow, looking at the painted image, it had never occurred to me that Stanford Lad could ever have been a puppy like other pups, big-footed, clumsy, and unlovely—or ever awkward or ever ignorant—no dog as dogs in my declining time were dogs, susceptible to love and fleas and uncouth toilet habits. It did not seem that ever Stanford Lad had walked at heel and been disciplined and hungry and cold and heir to evils of the flesh, that ever he had sickened and grown weak and feverish, his coat patchy and his eyes glazed, that purulence had shown upon that immortal nose, and the gaunt rib cage that housed his mighty heart had heaved desperately for breath and failed.

ALGONQUIN

You never thought it could be that way, but that was how it was. I sat up in bed, hugging my knees, and I could feel the age and the wisdom and the sadness, too, creeping over me like a chill, and I knew that I would never be quite so young and carefree as I had been a day before. Not only Stanford Lad but also Prime Minister. Had he ever died aflame, a shrieking dervish who laid a trail of fire across the prairie before he toppled dead, a charred, unrecognizable ruin of what had been a champion three times over?

And even High Valor? Could it be that even Val, whom Grandma called the Lord's own bird dog even while he lived—had life really touched him as it touched the rest? And envy, and malice, and treachery, and death? Had High Valor, greatest of his time, jerked witlessly upon the ground, an uncoordinated mass, slobbering loosely, perhaps weeping in his pain until, choked by a swollen tongue, he died?

And if it were truly so, then what of the man who had done it to him? Where was the man now, and how had he profited?

Old, I thought of me, old, old, old. I am getting old enough tonight that I will never need to count more birthdays. I lay down again, with my hands behind my head. My bedroom was not dark; outdoors I could see the last phase of the hunter's moon.

It would hang there, a little out of shape, all night and still glower from the horizon at sunup. Well, I would be all right. I would be calm and measured in my speech, modest in my bearing, and temperate in all things hereafter, for I felt myself come of age. I knew the family secrets now. It is not right for you to know too soon. They have to determine that you are brave. Now that I was adjusting myself, I was glad I knew. It was a man's duty to speculate upon what the future held for him. It was a good thing the dogs couldn't.

Suddenly I sat bolt upright again, the sweat popping out on my face. There had been a moment there, between sleep and waking, when I was just adrift and my mind made pictures that were almost dreams, and one of them was of Algonquin, the puppy, rising from his mother's dead grip—the way he looked upon the people waiting there, then turned and started back for the fire. He was different from other dogs; he knew too much. Maybe he did not have to speculate. Maybe something had spoken to him in the flames, telling him what he must do and how, and also how he must return and when. Maybe he knew what no man may know or ought to know.

After that, I could not sleep at all. It was nearly morning, and I dressed and went to the window, where I could look down on the wintering ground and the river and the marsh. While I stood looking out, there were shadows on the moon, and I could hear the signal bells of geese, an aerial convoy beating across the seas of air, ghost ships whose passage was enough to raise your hair at the hour of the owl, laying a straight course grimly from Nothing into Nowhere. There was the bell buoy of a gander on the river, and the armada swung responsively, turned into the wind, and, magnified by moonlight into titanic shapes, swirled down the long ladder from the stars and vanished in the darkness of the marsh.

I put on my coat and went downstairs and outside, down the hill, where the ridge ran out by running into the river. You could follow it for a long way, because it curled along and was the river-bank, where the river had been forced to swing out in order to get around it. There was a feeling of frost on the bluestem underfoot, and you could see your own breath whitely.

There was that strong half-light that made everything clear but without color, like a photograph, and the river was all silver, glittering. A rabbit popped out of its crab apple cafeteria and scrambled ahead of me a moment, as rabbits will, then became affected by the moon and developed a loose and drunken hop, pausing to sit up and look backward at me with solemn eyes but ears ridiculously askew.

I walked on down around the curve, keeping away from the bank because I could hear the mallard drakes, beeping over some melancholy flaw in mallard hens, down in the flaggers. Upriver, a goose spoke briefly on a subject of interest to all geese, and afterward the rest discussed his point in a subdued and courteous forum.

There was a log where the last slope of the ridge

met the first level of the marsh. I just sat there and listened. The hour of the owl passed, and the dimness of just-before-dawn came on, and in the moment before you could say it was getting light, the geese arose unseen and climbed their spiral staircase into heaven, and at the very top, where they leveled off, they came into the light and saluted it with trumpets and were gone. And at the last instant before the light soaked down to me, the greenheads clattered out of the flaggers along the high bank and moved up the river, the whistle of their pinions like the wind against closed shutters. And the last night sound there was came in the broken laughter of a loon, and, sitting there on the log, I thought I was going to cry.

But I didn't. There was the quick padding of a dog, and the dog came down the ridge where I had walked and came close to me and sat down.

Algonquin.

He startled me, because he had done a thing any dog might do.

"What do you want?" I asked him.

He didn't answer. It wouldn't have surprised me

much if he had. He sat there—it was light now—looking at me with a curious but still half-amused expression.

"Do you want it to be the way they say it will be?" I asked him. "I can stop it, you know. That's one thing I can do."

He looked at me, still curiously, but maybe not amused anymore.

"I could say that you are my dog and I want to take you home, and if I do, no one will stop me."

The amusement came back, brightening those golden eyes that watched me.

"I can, too," I said. "I could do that, and if I did, it would change a lot of things."

It was no use. I knew, and he knew, too, that Indian Maid hadn't come walking out of the fire that time for him to go home with me—not ever, ever, ever. And although it was true enough, what I could do, I knew and he knew that I would never do it. The tears were very close for me, and I reached out and put my arms around him, and for just a moment I could tell exactly how it would never be for me again with a dog, mortal and weak and

129

loving. Then he changed under my touch, going hard and strange and tight, and I took my arms away from him, and the moment that so seldom comes was gone.

Mr. Washington was coming down the hill. I moved over on the log and Mr. Washington sat down. After a moment, a red-winged blackbird behind us in the marsh recited the tinkling song he saves for his friends. The sun touched the oaks on top of the hill, so we could see the colors flare to life, and at the same moment, a squirrel called upon the world to witness some imaginary outrage within his dominions.

"Mighty pretty," Mr. Washington said. "I reckon there must be some reason most folks sleep away the best hours of their lives."

"Yes," I said. "Mighty pretty here."

"Reckon we better enjoy it while we can," said Mr. Washington. "Mr. Ovid, he letting it all go. Reckon they going ditch the marsh and plow it and plant wheat where the blackberries are. Won't be any more music in the morning then."

"No." I looked at Algonquin, sitting there with

his coiled grace, so ugly and still so beautiful, and I said to him, "Things that have been a certain way for a hundred years have to be changed, because you have a way of moving, and an old man has a way of looking, and I'm a coward."

"Things going to happen anyway," Mr. Washington said gently. "You might's well find a good reason to put onto it."

He paused a moment; then he said a grim thing. He said, "You might as well face it, boy; it's an awful responsibility a man has to a dog, after he's made the dog as much in his own image as he, his own self, is in God's."

I did not say anything. I was too appalled to speak. It couldn't be like that. Uncle Ovid was not bitter and sardonic; Uncle Ovid did not have the cold, freezing something in his eyes; Uncle Ovid didn't know too much about too much; not Uncle Ovid. No. It couldn't be that way.

Could it?

After a while Mr. Washington stood up, and I followed numbly. Instead of going back along the ridge, we cut through the wintering ground, where the red signal lights of blackberries flared now, and the bright thickets of the thorn apples and the purpling hazel, all over the haze of goldenrod and gamma underfoot.

Algonquin moved up beside Mr. Washington, sort of questioning. Mr. Washington put his hand above his head, not touching.

"You want to go; you make one cast, just one cast, you understand, if you want to go," and his hand gestured out, and I tell you that dog went. We were halfway through the wintering ground and Algonquin was maybe two hundred yards ahead, still breaking out wider, when he made game and veered around in a swing like a scythe, leaning but not slowing, and then he came down.

It was not like he had a covey of quail. It was something that resisted him, and he went in closer, hard and high and speaking to the bird in that magic and visible communication of a pointer.

And he shifted his weight like a swordsman and leaned forward, with that tight balancing power all drawing up into focus, so that his chest swelled and his head came up and his tail came up and the

muscles ridged along his shoulders, and you knew that the bird had understood his authority.

We walked it up, and it was a prairie chicken—one, all alone—and it burst upward and made one of the incomparable parabolas into the rising sun and was gone somewhere across the river.

"Time was," Mr. Washington said wistfully, "I was a boy, I crawl on my belly a mile through the marsh to get close enough to shoot without the sentries see me. Time was, when flocking-up time came, chickens get up out of here so it sound like thunder over behind the hills. Time was, when they out on the booming ground at sunrise, you wake up waiting for it to rain. Time was."

He shook his head.

"That all changing, too."

Up at the house, we went in the kitchen door, and Mrs. Washington had some breakfast ready: pancakes with fried eggs on top and side meat and maple syrup they had boiled down. She gave me a platter full of stuff, and I was eating pretty good, for a fellow who had put on so much age so fast, when Grandsir came downstairs.

He saw me and looked at me from under his eyebrows, but all he said was that I better finish up my packing because pretty soon we had to go home.

I did, and when I came down again, Grandsir and Uncle Ovid were back in the room with the wall of little windows. Grandsir evidently had been talking for some time but not the way he had talked the night before.

"You must understand, Ovid." He was dispassionate, like he was explaining a point of law to a jury. "I do not care so much about dogs anymore. But after you have been deeply involved with dogs, you do not stop remembering just because you have left them behind you."

"A man ain't got the right to leave a great dog behind him," Uncle Ovid said. "Not when all his life he's committed to giving a great dog everything he can, every time. As long as he's got dogs, he ain't got the right to hold out on a great one."

"There is no such thing as a great dog by himself," Grandsir said.

"No matter what you say." Uncle Ovid sounded very stubborn.

135

"Not by himself," Grandsir said. "A great dog is a symbol, a flag, a materialization of a man's will and the force of his spirit shaped in living flesh, molded in the image of perfection that other men have given up or compromised upon, the living dream of beauty that is such a bitter thing because each of us reaches a time when he knows in his heart that he will never be able to possess it."

"I guess you know," Uncle Ovid said. "I guess you know, all right."

"Yes, I guess I do." Grandsir was having quite a success keeping objective about this. "A great dog is born when a certain man and a certain dog come together and a spark is struck, so fierce and hot that the fire it kindles will not die until everything is burned away but the greatness."

"All right," Uncle Ovid said. "Don't I know all that?"

"Don't you?" Grandsir struggled a little, because his objectivity was slipping a little. Then he got it back. "Don't you know how much of your life you put into every dog and how much you are diminished when each one dies?"

136

"I don't want to know," Uncle Ovid said. "I'm an old man, and it wouldn't be good for me to know."

Grandsir almost felt sorry for him now. But not quite.

"I would not force it upon you, Ovid," he said. "I would not force it on you for the world."

"No." Uncle Ovid took a deep breath. "But I got a little left."

He waited, then said strongly, "I got a little left, I have. And I never—from a little boy—I never could bear to leave anything behind."

"Just so," Grandsir said. "It is much simpler when you can leave them behind, not caring so much for dogs anymore."

Uncle Ovid turned, with an odd expression on his face, and very, very quietly he asked, "How did that come about, Charleton?"

"A long time ago." Grandsir rose and straightened his coat. "All the care I had left over died in convulsions with High Valor and was buried with him, so he would never be alone. After High Valor there was nothing."

Afterward we went out and got in the rig, and

Mr. Washington drove us into town. For a long while Grandsir sat with his face down in his coat collar, and I sat thinking how he maybe had not told much about dogs, but he had said a true thing about men. Presently he straightened and looked at me. I smiled uncertainly, and he winked and put his big hand on mine and asked if there was anything I wanted to say, and I said, "Grandsir, I did not know your name was Charleton."

8

ALGONQUIN MIGHT HAVE BEEN READY the next year. Grandsir said he was readier than most dogs would ever be, but you don't ask that much of a spring derby. Peerless Mary went as far that way as any dog ought to go, and Grandsir said Uncle Ovid still had that much sense of perspective. With his third year coming on, though, they said you couldn't hold him back anymore. It was time, and everybody knew it was time.

Grandsir decided we'd stay home until after the partridge season, then go out and stay with Uncle Ovid on the circuit right through the finish in February. That way, I would lose quite a bit of school, but not nearly so much as I would if he didn't take me along and I carried out my threat to run away and become a cabin boy on a Mississippi steamer.

When our train got to the Junction, Mr. Washington wasn't there yet with the rig to pick us up. It was cold in the depot, so we walked across the street to the general store, and I had a dish of ice cream with maple sugar crumbled up on it. Grandsir stood up in front, looking out the window for Mr. Washington and nodding to different people. I knew some of them, too, by this time, like Mr. MacDonald, who ran the general store, and Dr. Westby, who, just then walking by, saw Grandsir through the window and stopped in.

"All set, Colonel?"

"Yes," Grandsir said. "All set, Wes."

"You haven't been out to the Old Place." Dr. Westby took out his pipe and filled it. He could have filled it with the tobacco he had spilled in the wrinkles of his vest the last time.

"No," Grandsir said.

"I have," Dr. Westby said. "He's a great dog, Colonel."

"Perhaps," Grandsir said. He looked almost casually at Dr. Westby's face, then looked out the window again. He said, "Although I don't suppose you went out to the Old Place to look at the dog."

140

"I understand the dog does not have much use for doctors," Dr. Westby said, "or anyone."

I sat there with a big gooey spoonful of ice cream halfway up to my open mouth. Dr. Westby wasn't a veterinarian. But before I figured out what that conversation meant, Dr. Westby shook hands with Grandsir and went out, and Mr. MacDonald went up close to Grandsir, where the gun rack was.

He took a gun down and wiped it carefully. It was not a new gun. It was a 28-gauge pump gun, and it had a hand-honed action so smooth that when you tipped the barrel up, the action worked by itself. He did that a few times, then put the gun back.

"It's a good gun," he said. "I cannot shoot the twenty-eight-gauge with justice anymore, Judge."

"You cannot live forever, either," Grandsir said. "There are some things a man might as well accept gracefully, since accept them, one way or another, he must."

"In my day—" Mr. MacDonald was wistful. He ran the store pretty steadily now that he was too old to stand a full day in the field. "Oh, in my day, though—"

It was all right for him to be wistful. A 28-gauge

141

is a very special kind of bird shooting gun. Grandsir used to say that a 12-gauge was for a realist, and a 20-gauge for the few who can shoot as well as they think they can, and a 16-gauge, which is the size in between, for the ones who are alarmed at taking a definite stand on anything. A .410, he said, was for braggarts, but the 28-gauge was for men who are artists in their souls, for the rare talents who can burn the picture of certain fabulous moments at the peak of a covey rise unforgettably into your memory. Mr. MacDonald had been that kind of shot, they said. Now he was old and a little stooped and kind of dusty-looking.

He said, not bragging, "Once I was a great shot, Judge. Some of the best shots I made over your great dogs. It was mighty nice to remember."

"Yes"—Grandsir did not turn around—"I suppose so."

"Then I was no longer a great shot," Mr. MacDonald said. "But, on the other hand, the days of the great dogs were gone, too, so I didn't feel bad."

Grandsir did not say anything. I felt my jaw going numb. They had caught me with another spoonful of ice cream halfway up to my mouth.

Mr. MacDonald said, "Now, though, it is different. Now it is different, all right. Now you have a great dog again." He paused and made a great effort. "But it is very plain that I will never make another great shot."

He put his hand on the 28-gauge gun in the rack for just a moment, very tenderly, but took it away as though it burned him.

"I am very restless," he said strongly, "but I don't begrudge you any of it, Judge."

"That's splendid," Grandsir said, "because I am very restless myself."

"Why, Judge," said Mr. MacDonald, "don't you remember how fine it was?"

"Oh, yes, indeed," Grandsir said savagely. "I remember very well. That is why I'm so restless."

Just then Mr. Washington pulled up in front with the rig and we went out, and we were a good mile out of town before I realized I still had the spoonful of ice cream in one hand, only the ice cream had melted and spilled all over my coat.

Mr. Washington was bundled up in a coat and kind of hunched over the reins. He did not offer to let me drive, and we rode along quite a while. Then Mr. Washington said, "Judge, I got to tell you something."

"No," Grandsir said.

"But I got to, Judge. Before we get there. The Old Place doesn't look the way it ought to, Judge. I got to tell you."

"No," said Grandsir.

"Don't you want to know, Judge?"

"No," said Grandsir. "But I know, anyway. You forget that we have been through this before."

"Yes, sir." Mr. Washington relapsed into his muffler. "I guess every time you got a great dog, you got the same old miseries all over again."

"No, George." Grandfather was having a very negative time. "With each one, the miseries are different."

Mr. Washington appeared to take some obscure comfort in that. I didn't. I finally came to and looked at the spoon. Then I wiped it off on my handkerchief and put it in my pocket, so I could return it, because if I didn't, Grandsir would make me pay for it out of my allowance. On my allowance, I calculated I wasn't prosperous enough to go throwing silver spoons around, even if they weren't silver.

Things had changed at the Old Place, for sure, this time. The lawn stood tall and uneven, with the nodding June grass heads up high in bunches over the vetch and fescue, and down at the ruins of the old kennel house, the bittersweet was reaching green fingers all the way across and climbing on the wire. The stables looked sort of abandoned, despite the presence of a couple of horses, but it was the big house that hurt you. It had not been painted now for a long while, and upstairs a blind had come loose on one hinge and broken a window, and the unhinged blind and broken window still were untouched. When we went up the steps of the porch, a loose board jumped, but Uncle Ovid did not seem to notice it. His white whiskers showed up stiff in bristles all the places they weren't usually, and his suit was rumpled and dirty.

He was very gay.

We went inside, and you could tell that no one really was devoting much attention to living there anymore. In the sitting room and the library, Mrs. Washington had put some slipcovers and white drapes over the furniture before she left, and in the other rooms the carpets were rolled up, and there were muddy tracks on the wide oak floors. Gear and hunting clothes and maps and entry blanks and premium lists and stuff like that littered everything and in some places spilled off on the floor and got walked on. I felt kind of funny, like I was snooping around in a place that maybe someone had just died in, only, of course, that was silly. Grandsir's face was dark and glowering, but when he spoke he sounded almost jovial, until you listened to what he said.

He said, "You're making fine progress, Ovid. The place begins to reek of poor whites and hound dog doings. Maybe we can scrape up a bait of chitlins," he went on, and I could feel the sharp edges of the sarcasm, "and later in the evening we can go out on the stoop and set and pass the jug and listen while the dogs start a coon."

He stamped out into the kitchen, still raging, then stopped short.

The dog was lying on a quilt beside the kitchen couch, which clearly was where Uncle Ovid slept. Grandsir looked at him and Algonquin looked back,

cool and a little amused, as usual, but somehow harder than he used to be, as though his wonderful restraint was stretching a little thin and maybe pretty soon it would give way, and whatever that strange, strange thing was, frozen deep in his eyes, would thaw out and stretch and rise upward until it stared you right in the face.

"Well," Grandsir said in an entirely different tone. "Well, Ovid."

Algonquin put his head back down on his forepaws and did not look at us anymore. I want to tell you, there never was a dog like Algonquin. He sprawled there, with idle grace, upon a quilt my great-grandmother had quilted with her own hands as a girl in Boston and carried across the wilderness in a Conestoga wagon, a quilt that had been in the walnut bedroom and had kept the cold from generals and congressmen and judges and maybe even the man who almost was President once, when Grandsir was a boy and people like that used to come to the Old Place. The big white dog with the devil's head spread himself on it, and I don't know as any of the people who had used it before had been more impressive using it than he was. It was there in the gloomy and musty stale-food-smelling kitchen with the old-fashioned cypress sink and the hand pump and the wood range and the rumpled couch. It was a thing you couldn't name, like a light shining on him, cold with the spiritual cold that chills your heart but is impersonal and not good or evil that you could tell.

I tell you, that dog would have raised your hair just by being in the room with you. He did not care about anything, one way or another; he just disregarded it, dismissed it, or ignored it entirely. He did not pay any particular attention when you tried to talk to him, but he knew when you started to talk about him and what you said and what you meant—and then something that I never actually knew but only felt, as though maybe he knew how what you were talking about would come out, or not come out, and there would be a feeling of laughter around him, like something was a dreadful, mocking joke.

Uncle Ovid said softly, "I reckon that will be all the talk of hound dogs."

"Yes." Grandsir's voice was just as quiet. "That will be all."

149

Uncle Ovid walked into the kitchen, standing taller and straighter than I remembered, and despite the untidy way he was dressed, he looked more like Grandsir than I ever saw him.

"However, you must forgive the condition of the premises, Charleton," Uncle Ovid said gracefully. "No one is left to help now. But it does not matter—there is not so much to help with."

He smiled warmly and added, explaining, "Mr. Washington is busy outdoors, and, of course, I do not have time, Charleton."

Uncle Ovid seemed to have a little of that cold white light around him, too. Grandsir was silent, and Uncle Ovid said, "You were right: I do not have enough time. I am getting very short of time now, Charleton."

Grandsir said, "A man does what he has to do."

At that, Uncle Ovid straightened up even taller and smiled, really meaning it for a smile this time. It lasted just a moment before the big white dog raised his head and stared at Uncle Ovid with those freezing eyes, and it was as though he said something, although, of course, he didn't, but Uncle Ovid stopped smiling.

150

"That's very fine of you, Charleton. I thought you would reproach me for how I squander my little time. I recall how harsh you were with me when it first became a possibility."

"That was different. I still might have saved you," Grandsir said. "Now it would be unjust. A man is entitled to make his own bargains and to pay for them. Freedom of conscience is a precious concept in the interpretation of the law, and a free man has an inalienable right to his tears of regret at the ruin to which he brings himself."

"I think you have been a very fine jurist," Uncle Ovid said.

Grandsir said, "I have been very devoted to the law."

That's all there was to that. When Grandsir and I went up to bed, I stayed very close to him. There was a feeling in the house that made me want to stay close to someone. There was dust everywhere upstairs; you could track yourself around as though you were walking in snow. It was my room where the window was broken, and that made a dandy excuse for me to follow Grandsir into his room. That was on the same side of the house as mine was, so I didn't escape anything, after all. There was moonlight again from a swollen, lopsided moon, and, although I had been trying to avoid doing it ever since we arrived, I could not help looking out the window across the acres that spread to infinity.

There was a vast, misshapen, ugly bulk of machinery down in the marsh, and even by moonlight you could see the ugly scars of ditching and the black emptiness of earth where the wintering ground had been and where the bulldozers were leveling now for crops. I knew it would be that way, but it hurt, anyway, and after I had shown myself it was as bad as I imagined, I turned away.

Grandsir said to me, "Boy, you want to watch all this carefully from now on."

"No, I don't," I said. "I don't want to watch it at all."

"Oh, but you must watch carefully just the same," Grandsir said. "What happens now will not be pretty, but it will be very informative."

The next day we were up early, and Uncle Ovid was impatient to get through with breakfast so we could go out and see Algonquin work. When we came back, Grandsir rode with his head down and his hands clasped on the saddle horn. Mr. Washington took the horses, and we stood for a moment in front of the stable. Uncle Ovid had that same look of feverish excitement about him, only it was stronger today.

Grandsir said slowly, "Well, it is a strange thing. You cannot get any more out of a dog than you put into him."

Uncle Ovid gestured, as though to brush away that part.

"Well, what do you think, Charleton?" he asked triumphantly.

"Ovid, Ovid." Grandsir's voice was so quiet and so sad it made my lip quiver. "Ovid, my brother," he said like a chant, "Ovid, Ovid, what have you done?" But no one really knew.

III

"There is a poem you might want to look up after a while," Grandsir said. "It might help you think of the questions that you'll have the answers to."

"Oh," I said, "is it a poem about a dog?"

"No," said Grandsir, "it is a poem about a Tyger."

9

WHATEVER IT WAS that you had to put into a dog to make him great, and wherever you had to take it from, Uncle Ovid did it. As I remember the judgment of my elders, there was no doubt about Algonquin. Afterward, men who had seen him measured the excellence of other dogs by saying, "There is one who looks like Algonquin." And you then could pick out the ones who really had known Algonquin, I mean known him well, because they would look at each other then and smile and shake their heads, because there never was a dog like Algonquin.

But you heard such things only occasionally and on days of great enthusiasm, when a very good dog in a very lucky heat would accomplish climactically, just that once, what Algonquin did always, easily and with reckless abandon.

The main thing I remember was how it seemed a pity to ask any common dog to run against him, because he was more than a dog inside, more than any dog ought to be, and you'll have to decide for yourself what it was that made him that way. It was a feeling you had after first watching him, and after you knew him awhile, it was stronger, but it changed, too, so that you began to feel it was a pity to ask any common man to handle a dog against him, as well.

Not that he was any trouble. He was not sullen or mean or bad-hearted. He was not like Muscle Shoals Jake, who was so thorough about not liking things that they had to put the livestock up in trees when he came by. No, Algonquin was as merry as any trial judge could ask, but it was a devilish gaiety, and the fuel he drew on to keep it bright came from that wonderful, glittering, inexhaustible cold thing that sort of frosted you when you looked into his eyes.

I had a very difficult time expressing what I thought, even to myself, until one day after we had watched him Grandsir said, as much to himself as to me, "Behold the consuming rage, and the rest is ashes."

158

This was another of the things Grandsir said that confused me, and, although I did not understand exactly what he meant, I knew I must cling desperately to that phrase, because it would mean something eventually.

Right then, I knew it meant Algonquin hated something. The thing was, you did not know what it was he hated. At different times it seemed different things, and just when you were about sure, you advanced a little in your understanding of him and realized that you had been entirely wrong and this was another thing he did not really hate; but he hated something, all right.

At first a lot of men thought he hated people, because he looked at them with curdling contempt and looked past them, as though they were not there. Some of them were hurt, and some were angry, but they needn't have been, because he did not really hate people. It was that he knew the things men wanted and the things they did and what they were worth, maybe, but he couldn't help them, and they couldn't help him—no one at all could help him—so he did not pay any attention to people anymore.

159

Then, after the first of the big trials, there was a good deal of talk about how he hated the other dogs, how he wanted to destroy them, and how that was the reason that he very nearly did destroy several of them—not directly, of course, but with his impeccable and relentless way of destroying them little by little in the field, by obliterating the self-respect that a winner must have.

You put him down with a dog, and the first part of the heat he spent finding out just what the other dog's limit was, in speed and range and sight and wind. And after that, he did everything just a little bit beyond the other dog's utmost ability and did it in a way you knew was breaking the other dog's heart. When he had done that and made his bracemate into a broken and dispirited trailer hardly going through the motions anymore, he took his graceful farewell and went out ahead to his main performance for the two judges and the gathered gallery.

In the bylaws of many field trial clubs, the championship is to be awarded to the Open-All-Age dog who, on a certain day, most closely approaches the ideal of a shooting dog for purposes of actual hunting under similar field conditions. That is a noble precept in some eyes, and progressively closer adherence to it in the years of my time is why we have seen emerge the unlovely concept of the meat dog and the even less savory emphasis on birds by the pound. It also probably is why no one cares so much about dogs anymore. For in the time before my time, bird dogs were brought to a very high pitch, and the people who produced them knew it and provided a shooting-dog stakes, in which the shooting dogs were run and judged as you judge any other workman's effectiveness at his trade.

But in that time, when everyone held an ideal of perfection in his mind and a great many people cared a very great deal about dogs, an Open-All-Age dog was a different thing. There were no rigid definitions of what he should do but only of the effect he should create. That was because poetry fits very loosely in formal regulations, and an Open-All-Age dog was a thing of poetry. He was a sort of wisp of pure splendor, given momentary substance within a frame of ritual, like a sonnet or the decathlon or the Order for Burial of the Dead.

We make many parables in our world now to

keep our love of beauty from ourselves. An Open-All-Age bird dog was one of the first and most open of them, and learning to appreciate the genius of his spirit was one of the most difficult and desirable attainments of a mysterious and almost vanished culture. He was a little like a virtuoso with a violin, doing many fabulous things and showing you while he was doing them why you would never see it done in just such a way again. Perhaps he was even more like a great conductor, because he dominated a whole orchestra of parts, he mastered the formal environment of the trial, and he included the acoustics of emotion in his song. He bent the participants to his will, and he drew passages out of even the mediocre that could not be equaled again under any circumstances, and he put upon the best of them a little of his own magic before he turned to another movement of his program and mercifully allowed the spotlight to be drawn from their exhausted faces.

That was Algonquin, and if you ever saw him, you know what I mean. You saw that he did not hate the other dogs, and a famous judge, who was very old even then, was one of the first to see it.

After the heat, he rode around and said to Uncle Ovid, "The dog is very gallant, sir; I think perhaps he would pity his bracemates if he were not enough of a nobleman to know they would rather die than be pitied."

When you saw how just and reasonable that was, you knew that the other dogs were not what he hated, because he did the best he could for them, too. He was letting them show their best, because he could not help what he had to do to them afterward. It was not his fault that they were so much less than he that the comparison sickened even them, and it was the pride he had in himself that made him do the same things himself, so beautifully and arrogantly and with something so splendid in the air around him that the other dog could not endure it but broke in tragic disgrace and, for the rest of the heat, went around pointing meadowlarks, because that way Algonquin would stay away from him.

And most certainly he did not hate the birds. He had the feeling for the birds that they all have, that is the foundation of their art. The birds are the medium of a bird dog, and he must be united with them in his heart, and understand them, and be trusted by them, and speak through his artistry and control them with the power of his genius, or he has lost the frame of ritual—he no longer fulfills the fiction of convention—he is adrift and nothing.

The birds were where Algonquin was unmatched. He spoke to them in the immortal and universal language that all men and all dogs understand, and the galleries would hush to hear the rolling periods of his classic declamation. When you saw him swinging wide, burning whitely across the bird fields with that blazing speed, to come down on a full wild covey in a locked and statuesque point that skidded him ten yards, pinwheeling across the stubble on braced legs, lofty as a king acknowledging the presence of other royalty, you knew that you had seen what painters see in their hearts but seldom put on canvas.

But it was the other times, the rare and unexpected times, when circumstance called upon the resources of his originality, that you felt the hush come down on the gallery, and even the horses paused. It was like this when his bracemate was very lucky very early and made a splendid find, and Algonquin

164

came to back him and backed him with that high-stationed pride, saluting the other dog's work in a tribute so fine that the white light of magic descended on him and blinded you, and you could not remember afterward what the other dog had done, but you remembered Algonquin.

There was the time when the gallery was very eager to watch him and followed much too closely on the judges. Uncle Ovid spoke to the marshal, and the marshal turned them, but some riders were so eager they pulled away to one side and galloped along a little ridge, and that was where the course turned, and they were in the path of the coursing. The dog who was down with Algonquin accepted the error and turned away from the horses, but Algonquin went into them and through their groups, and with them all around him, he made game. One of the judges said something very sharp and began to spur his horse toward Algonquin, but there was no haste.

There, with the uneasy horses and embarrassed riders pulling back, Algonquin moved in on his bird tenderly. The judges rode in and looked at him very seriously, then motioned to Uncle Ovid, and

Uncle Ovid dismounted and walked in.

No bird rose, and the gallery groaned a little, just a sighing sound of disappointment, but Uncle Ovid stooped and picked up a cock quail that was very calm and unalarmed because Algonquin had spoken to him as no dog ever spoke before. Uncle Ovid walked a little way and held up his hand, and bobwhite came back from the far land where he had been resting his spirit and was very frightened suddenly and flew wildly and desperately out through the line of horses, and there was the long hiss of breath through the gallery that meant more than the applause coming afterward.

There was another time when the judge first said, "Let them go!" and the brace went as they always go when they have the terrible energy bottled up in them and it is released, and Algonquin stretched out ahead and suddenly cartwheeled, as though something had reached up from the ground and caught him by the head, and it had. A find on barren ground is a wonderful thing, but most handlers fear it, because it is so shocking that it may jar the artist in a bird dog out of place, and for just a moment he is all dog. That is where you see

166

handlers smoking their dogs to hold them or slapping their crops pointedly against their boots walking in, and those things are not very nice, either. But Algonquin made the point in full stride, and his bracemate, who was running very desperately, trying to catch up, came through too fast and blasted the stray single out and hardly recovered in time to steady at wing, but Algonquin stood there.

This was the quality of his manners in the presence of game, and afterward men who knew him used it as a measure, so you can see, whatever it was he hated, it was not the birds.

I have told you these were the great days. I guess we hit most of the trials. That doesn't matter. Even though I was only a boy, I realized it did not matter whether I remembered the names, because there are more important things to remember about great days. If it is only the names you want, and the performance records, you can stay at home and read them in a book, and you will know all there is to know about them except the part that really matters. Grandsir did not have to tell me about that, because when you are a kid, you know it better and have more confidence in knowing it than you will again

167

until you are very old and wise and have experimented with the other ways.

It is being there that matters, being full of hot grits and side meat and so cold that the rest of you is jealous of the belly being warm, so cold you sit on the horse and shiver until you think maybe you better hang on to the saddle, but that isn't dignified, and the dew on the handlers' boots and the jingle of harness and the horses moving a little restlessly and the electric feeling before a brace is cast off, even if they are not good dogs. Of course, on the circuit, they all are very good dogs, but they do not always have very good days. Field-trial performances depend on many things. They depend on the bracemate you draw and the time of day and whether there was a good dew and whether you are working over a section where other dogs were put down previously, so that the coveys are scattered and scared. Those things all are important, and sometimes they make a great deal of difference, but Algonquin did not care about them. Of course, when he was lucky, too, and drew an early heat and the dew and several big coveys and a fine bracemate, those were the really magnificent days, when everyone on the field knew he was witnessing an event.

Those days affected me very strongly, and at the end of them I felt drained and exhausted, and even though I was not such a little boy anymore, I felt fretful and might have wept easily if there were anything definite to weep about. One time, I remember, I went to sleep in the saddle, and the horse kept moving, and Grandsir came after me, and I woke up when he took hold of my bridle.

"You're very tired, boy, aren't you?"

"Yes, sir," I said sleepily.

"But now we have started this, and we must see it through," Grandsir said. "Just remember, someday all this will seem very long ago."

10

W E," UNCLE OVID SAID, always "we."

That meant he was speaking of Algonquin and himself. He did not say "I" anymore, or "he," but only "we." It was a thing you didn't notice at first; then it insinuated itself into your attention, and you tried to ignore it, but you noticed it even more intensely then, straining your senses for new manifestations of it and dreading to find them. In the field, you saw it work; the tall old man and the white dog did not need any apparent communication. More than once I have seen Algonquin carry a cast to the outermost limit of judgment and be turned, as though you turned him by force, when my uncle did not even gesture, much less whistle, but willed that he should turn.

And once I was close enough to see how, at the

end of a heat, when a handler may call upon a famous champion to finish with a mighty final sweep against the odds of time and fatigue, my uncle stood still and closed his eyes, and his whole body tensed in a gathering motion, and the veins swelled on his forehead with the effort but not for himself. Instead, when he let his breath out explosively, it was Algonquin, a quarter mile away, who hurtled forward in a climactic drive as memorable as the falling of a star.

And time after time I saw them, in the gray light of morning, the man kneeling beside the dog with the bizarre head, at the hour when, during the long campaigns, a champion feels the universal mortality of all flesh, and his blood runs slow and the throat is thick and the fire of the spirit is banked with sheer weariness. I have seen Uncle Ovid, his face gray as the dawn, kneel beside the dog on the line and speak to him softly, and the dog would look at him, hardly caring. But my uncle would talk rapidly and tenderly, and the dog would change slowly under the effect not of the language but of the man's determination, and the increasing glow of mockery and bitterness would rise in his chilling yellow eyes, the cold light of rage would puff into life and blaze higher, and the power would surge through the gaunt body again, and when the hoarse voice cut through the expectant hush saying, "Cast them off, gentlemen," Algonquin would go, just as he always went, more dog than any dog should ever be, tireless and unrelenting.

But Uncle Ovid would not be that way. Even in the beginning, he would come back slowly from the line and his feet would drag wearily, as though it were late afternoon instead of morning, and during the heat he would stoop, and the lines would deepen in his face, as though he were running it himself, instead of the tall white dog. There was a time when he still knelt when the dogs were hunting their way far out, and Grandsir started forward because it did not seem my uncle would rise to his feet unaided.

"Never mind, Charleton." Uncle Ovid's voice would be weak, but you could see him summoning up new reserves of strength. "Never mind. See how we already are on the horizon."

He meant Algonquin was there.

Then, by night, Uncle Ovid would be very pale and weak. You get to know the other handlers of the big-time dogs. They live in a little world alone, and because Uncle Ovid was very old and had been very famous when most of them were little boys, they were kind. Of course, he was an owner, too, and that made some difference, but even without that he was very impatient. There was nothing wrong with him that being kind could help, he said. Mostly, he wanted to rest. Grandsir would sit and talk to him until he went to sleep, and the white dog slept on the floor beside him. Sometimes my uncle stirred in his sleep and muttered, and the white dog would raise that head with the chilling, sleepless eyes and look at him, not loving or sentimental or even as though it mattered one way or another, but knowing the desperate extent of their alliance.

Grandsir would tiptoe away then and shake his head and say something I could not understand because it was in some foreign language.

Once Uncle Ovid heard and woke up.

"What's that, Charleton?" He propped himself on his elbow and repeated, "What did you say?"

"I did not really say it." Grandsir hardly ever was sharp with Uncle Ovid now. Mostly he was sort of waiting.

173

"I heard you," Uncle Ovid said. "Quoting Simonides, in Greek. 'Tell them in Lacedaemon, passerby, that here, obedient to their word, we lie.' "

Grandsir did not say anything, and after a moment Uncle Ovid relaxed again.

"You do not have to worry, Charleton. Maybe we have gone out one time too many. Maybe we will use up the last mysterious supplies of our mutual time." He gave a peaceful kind of sigh here and said, "But you remember, Charleton, I was very wasteful in my youth. We can go back and gather up the fragments of courage and strength discarded then, and we will last them out; we will last all right."

Grandsir sounded as though he would rather not say it but had to. "Until when, Ovid?"

"That's a very good question, Charleton," he said and folded his hands on the cover and went back to sleep.

I might have been considerably more worried about the latter part of that conversation if I had not been stalled over the first part. To begin with, I was astonished that Uncle Ovid recognized the Greek and knew what it was, and I wondered if maybe he did not know a great many things like that but did not want to admit knowing them. And I wondered also what it was in a man which made him deprecate his own knowledge, because, goodness knows, no matter how much you have, it amounts to very little.

Then I thought about Algonquin and how they talked about what he was and how he got that way, and something kept bothering me, and I wondered whether it is not possible that when you are very old and very wise and know so very much, you might have forgotten just a little. There is something in a boy, an instinct that trusts in sorcery and spells and unspoken prophecies, and the something that is gone before a boy becomes a man had spoken to me in the night—that night Algonquin came alone out of the fire, then turned and desired to go back in— and I thought that perhaps Algonquin had been the way he was before they knew what he would be. I wondered whether the rage that was in him came from their stopping him when he wanted to go back into the fire, but I could not imagine how that might be possible, and I thought also, in a confused and feverish way, that I would know, if I could remember whether that buried light had been in his yellow eyes before, or only after.

Sitting there half-asleep, I reached that point and jumped in fright and turned my head. Uncle Ovid was asleep and Grandsir was sunk in meditation, but Algonquin was watching me with that unspeakable stare, and I swear I thought he would laugh, and the laugh would be too full of rage and bitterness for anyone to bear.

But, of course, he didn't, and Grandsir stirred and glared at me and made me go to bed, where I belonged.

After it was over, no one remembered when it started. A dog in competition has his own flesh and blood to contend with, and it is very hard because of the demands he makes. His feet get so hard they are like leather, so tough you could hardly cut them with a knife, but he wears his nails so short sometimes they bleed after a long run on hard ground, and, of course, the brambles always are there, cutting fine gashes across the loins and under the forelegs. It gets so a dog's muzzle is bare and nearly raw between nose and eyes, just from hitting cover, and the hair is all worn off around the eyes. Then the weed seeds get in his ears and eyes, and some-

176

times you don't get them all washed out with the borax water at night, and then there is trouble. Or the seeds and pollen and things like that are so heavy some days, and he gets his nose and throat clogged with them and has to cough every little while, only he won't take time to do it while he's running but saves all the coughing and wheezing for afterward, until you think he's going to die any minute. It is a hard life, and it is not mastered by qualities you teach to any dog. He has it bred into him for thousands of years by elimination and for several hundred additionally on purpose, and either it comes down to him strongly enough so nothing stops him or it does not; and there's no use trying to teach him any more than there is trying to make him forget it if you do not want him to have it.

These hardships came to Algonquin, just as they happen to any trial dog. He did not care; he did not even notice, and he seemed to sneer at us when we took care of his cuts and injuries. That's why it was so hard afterward to tell when the cough started.

It was nothing at first; you did not notice. There was a regional championship, I remember. It was a hot day, and they put the money dogs down in a three-hour heat, which is the same long grind they have in the final series of the Free-for-All and the National. Algonquin was down with a bitch who was middling fair but was very smart and figured things out for herself very quickly. After that, she ran as though she had drawn a bye and worked busily on whatever he left her, and although, as I said, she was middling fair, Algonquin was so wide and so fast and so sure that it looked like she was misplaced and ought to be running in the foot stakes with the Irish setters and the Brittanies. Of course, he did not put on his performance for nothing. He took what he had and brought it out, and it was just that he had so much to give that illuminated it with the authenticity of being so much to see.

At the end of the heat, there was a long hill, and the judges were waiting off at one side, and the marshal was at the end with a handsome roan horse, and Uncle Ovid called on Algonquin for one more long cast, the finish everyone waited for. He made it, a flat-racing, white sickle, curving across the field of sedge in that wonderful symmetrical pattern he had, soaring like the last four bars of a symphony and loud with the timpani that each man heard for

himself, in the pulse thudding in his own ears.

But when Uncle Ovid brought him back to the wagon, he was coughing—a dry, hard, hacking cough, and you noticed it then, all right.

No one said anything; no one dared mention it. The next day, instead of waiting for the rest of the braces, we went out alone, and Uncle Ovid put him down again. This time, without the competition to fire him, it did not take so long. The cough frightened me dreadfully; I did not know anything about it, but I was very frightened, because it seemed I could feel how it hurt; and the way his ribs heaved through the tight skin, as though he could not breathe, and, worst of all, the way he looked afterward, the eyes yellow and malevolent with rage that had burst into flower and was there in the open now for anyone to see. You could see the object of his hate there now, indistinct, but coming closer now, closer to the surface, and evil, evil, as though he were getting ready for what he had known all along was coming and which now was very near.

We did not even wait to get the trophy and have Algonquin's picture taken with it and mark down the names of the men who wanted to get pups by him when the time came. We went right on to the next city, because Uncle Ovid did not want to start the talk that getting a local veterinarian would do.

In the city, Uncle Ovid and Grandsir and Algonquin went into the vet's place and left me waiting in the office. I must have sat there all morning, alone, watching people with sick dogs come in and wait and tire of waiting and go out. After a while another doctor came in hastily and went in where Uncle Ovid and Grandsir and Algonquin were. Then, still later, I heard Uncle Ovid shouting something terrible, a long way down the halls, and one doctor came out looking mad and a little disheveled, and a new one came in from outside.

But I guess all the shouting in the world couldn't help. You could see that, by looking at Uncle Ovid and Grandsir.

They looked like two men who had lived too long and done too many things and were too exhausted to do whatever there was left for them to do. I understood why Uncle Ovid was that way, sick, but Grandsir did not care so much about dogs anymore, so he must have been sick from something else.

181

11

No ONE EVER TOLD ME any more about what happened there. We loaded up and started on the road, and I knew we were going home. Mostly, Grandsir and Uncle Ovid were very polite to each other and very gentle to me and were kind of not there at all the rest of the time. Mr. Washington and I did whatever needed to be done, and by the time we were settled back at the Old Place, I was about as old as Mr. Washington was when we started out, and Grandsir and Uncle Ovid were only a little bit younger than God.

At the Old Place, it was late winter. There still was snow on the north sides of the shelterbelt evergreens and ice in the pools where the river overflowed during thaws, but during the middle of the day the ground was soft, and the second day I found a pasqueflower on the bar, and the day after that I was lifted right out of my bed just at dawn by the trumpet call of geese.

Around the house for a few days I walked on tiptoe, because I did not want to make any noise and disturb Uncle Ovid and Grandsir, who appeared to be listening very hard for something.

But presently it seemed that you couldn't hold your breath anymore, and for a little while Uncle Ovid and Grandsir did not listen so hard. One night it turned cold and froze the puddles and the drenched grass, and afterward it snowed.

In the morning Mr. Washington went out and stocked his bird feeder, the one that stood on a stump cut high for the purpose, so you could see it from the window beside the fireplace. For a long time there were no birds. Then a cardinal cock swooped down to it, looking like a flame against the snow. Two blue jays came along, conducting a transient quarrel, saw the cardinal in the feeder, and promptly began shouting, "Thief! Thief!" in unison, even though they knew the cardinal would leave all the suet for them.

I focused the glass on him to see whether he was

the same bird Uncle Ovid banded after an accident three years before. He wasn't. A new cardinal was cock of the hill now. The blue jays were in good voice. Then I saw a downy woodpecker, who was inspecting the hickory tree beside the stable. The jays attracted him, and he came over to see what they were shrieking about. When he landed on the roof of the feeder and tuned up with a couple of preliminary rattles, the brightest sparrow of them all gave up trying to get his breakfast in the feeder and flew away. So did the downy, back down the hill where the poison ivy grew, which Uncle Ovid once had spent all spring cutting back so the downies could reseed it from the berries they loved in the winter. The poison ivy had gotten fierce the last couple of years, though.

The birds made me feel better. They reminded me that outside our house the world was busy, and the end of certain personal great days comes with the same kind of sunset that ends any other day. It even made me think that in some ways it was a good thing that the great days did not last forever, because no one would appreciate them then, or understand them, or maybe even be able to stand them, because you are not conditioned to endure great days forever. Possibly not at all.

The snow around the feeder was marked by tracks, bird tracks. What kind of tracks would they be, I wondered, if there were no birds? That made me smile a little to myself, because if I had said it aloud, Grandsir's eyebrows would have wrenched into a comical slant, and he would have allowed that either I was a very backward boy, or else I was very bright and likely should grow up to be a conspicuously bad poet.

Anyway, it was time to go outside and walk in the snow. Grandsir put on his coat and came along, because there is a feeling you get in fresh snow, and that was going to be the last snow of the winter. There is no use wasting anything like that. We did not go out the front of the house, because out there, where the wintering ground and the marsh used to be, the land looked naked and desolate, even under the snow. The snow healed the scars made by the bulldozers and covered the welts of ditches, but it was like a cemetery, just the same, and you have to be in a certain kind of mood before you go wandering around in snow-covered cemeteries.

185

Instead, we left Uncle Ovid sitting in the chair in front of the wall, where the windows were curtained now, so you did not need to look out and see how the end of something marched across the prairie at you, and went out in back. We crossed the grove of oaks, making our own tracks in the snow, and, along the edge of the woods, looked for other tracks. There was a brush pile, and when I jumped on it a rabbit burst frantically from the far side and dashed headlong into the woods, throwing little divots of snow spray behind him. Farther along, there was a set of tracks like rabbits with bare feet, only there was a tail, sometimes making a series of dents like maybe the owner had a complaint or two to make and emphasized them with his tail. We followed the tracks to where their owner had dug a nut out of a hollow stump and gone back up a tree. He sputtered indignantly after we passed, and I thought how if all the squirrels were gone, the woods would lose many qualities that at first glance do not seem to have to do with squirrels.

On the edge of the pasture, there was a belt of standing hay, and snow had bowed it over, and the miniature mountain range of grass was cobwebbed

186

with the complicated tunnels of field mouse engineers arising early.

We encountered the long trail of a venturesome mouse surveyor aiming at the woods. Here was a tail to be reckoned with, furrowing between the birdlike tracks. We followed him as he made his tour, bent on some microtomic research, and observed how he had been set upon by fate. We tracked him from clump to clump, losing him once in a while where he'd dawdled and backtracked around a ragweed stalk, to the ambush where the weasel had lain in wait. The weasel's body had melted a depression behind his screen of grass, and I imagined him licking his villainous chops at the prospect of fresh mouse steaks.

There was a climax where the weasel sprang, and the traces of a flurry in the snow. But it was all right. The next mouse tracks were a good three feet away and kept going, wide-spaced with haste and lacking the dalliance of tail marks. The weasel tracks followed but didn't catch up. Our adventurer had made it the ten feet to the rock pile. Many weasel tracks and angry scratches testified to his safety.

"Well," Grandsir said, "it is not always the same

story. This one turned out to have a happy ending."

"Not for the weasel," I said.

Grandsir stopped and rubbed his face thoughtfully.

"That is a rare thing, boy; that is one of the things a boy is so clever about but a man is afraid to face."

We started back to the house, and after we had walked halfway, Grandsir shook his head again and said, "Yes, indeed, boy, a basic truth. Every time a mouse escapes, a weasel goes hungry; therefore, what is a happy ending?"

"I don't know," I said. "I was just asking."

That is a thing about snow. You go out in it, and if you look about you, it is easy to become involved with many of your neighbors in the wild community; you become interested, and even concerned, and presently you realize that what you are seeking is, truly, a morsel of comfort in animal analogues, a reassurance of your own mighty fate from the small fates of field mice.

Then either you are embarrassed and stop looking so closely, or you are not embarrassed, and then you had better be careful. Because if you keep looking,

188

sooner or later you may be forced to admit that the prophecies of nature are written very brutally in bloodstains on the snow and proclaim how many must die so some may live, making mercy a temporary waste and power eventually vain. Then you might as well go where there is no snow anymore, to save yourself from brooding, unless you like to brood.

But after the walk in the snow, Grandsir and I came in and cleaned our boots and started into the other room but could not get by because Algonquin was lying in the doorway, his head down on his forepaws. The yellow eyes were open and glowing with the rage that had begun to ripple and boil on the surface lately, and while we stood there thinking about stepping over him, his flews curled savagely and contemptuously, but he was not looking at us; those tortured eyes were looking into another time.

"He still sneers," Grandsir said. "The mutinous spirit, knowing it must die."

"Will he die, Grandsir?"

"Yes," Grandsir said. "But so must we all. It is a thing you have to get used to, boy."

"I guess maybe he knew it all along," I said.

"Be that as it may," said Grandsir. "Then he knew as much as any man. There is a scriptural injunction, that you must be ready at any time to render up your stewardship and present an accounting of your term."

"Sir," I said, "what is it that no one is supposed to know about dying?"

Grandsir really looked at me now.

"Not the day or the hour or the manner of it, boy."

"Then that is what he knew," I said, and I knew when I said it that my voice was shaking a little with hysteria. "He knew it all along, and so did I."

"Well, now." Grandsir put his hand on my shoulder and let his breath out so it was loud. "And how did you know, boy?"

"You told me," I said, and he had, although he did not remember; he had told me when he spoke the names of great dogs, when he described the bond between men and dogs; he had told me in the lines of sadness on his face when everyone else was flushed with triumph; he had told me by knowing more about men and dogs than he would ever tell; he had told me by not telling. I could not possibly explain, but he had told how it would be, and when, in intimate detail: the story of the life and death of great Algonquin, in a parable concerning how everything is for nothing, and worth every bit of it.

12

Spring came on quickly that year. Sometimes it seemed that Algonquin was all right, around the house and in the yard, but he could not work anymore without bringing on the cough, and that was such a terrible thing to see that after it happened once or twice accidentally, everyone was very careful to see that it should not happen anymore.

No one said anything about the trials, from the time we came home. I marked off the days in my mind, and the day the Free-for-All started I knew it, but around the Old Place it was as though there was no place like Shuqualak and no state like Mississippi and no such thing as a bird dog anymore.

Two weeks later was when the travelers would be converging on Grand Junction, the fine dogs and the famous handlers and the owners and the people who wanted to be owners or tried to be handlers or had that strange yearning inside of them that made them look at bird dogs. By that time, though, I had convinced myself the days would pass unnoticed, and I went to bed as usual.

Then suddenly someone was shaking me awake, and it was Uncle Ovid. The lamp he held flickered from the draft, but I could see he was dressed in his fine boots and breeches and the split coat with the velvet lapels, his moustache trimmed and his face flushed. I was all confused from being asleep and dreaming, and I blubbered something incoherent, but Uncle Ovid smiled and said gaily, "Why, boy, rise and shine. In two hours they put down the first dogs in the National."

I was very bewildered and not sure even whether I was awake or still dreaming. Sitting up in bed, I stammered out a question about whether he thought Algonquin was going to win, after all.

"Why, boy," Uncle Ovid said fiercely, "he never lost at nothing, and he isn't going to start now."

He left me the lamp then and went downstairs, and I got dressed numbly, with the fog of unreality swirling around me, because, after all, we were five hundred miles from Tennessee, and Algonquin could not run a hundred yards. But Uncle Ovid said so and looked so, and when I started downstairs, I could smell the ham and potatoes and coffee that meant a field breakfast was ready. Mr. Washington was working busily over the range, like in the old days, when his wife was away, and Algonquin lay on the quilt beside the couch, sprawled carelessly and watching us. He looked nearly as good as ever, as strong and confident, and he was breathing all right except for a little catch that stirred his ribs once in a while, but he looked different, too, although I could not tell right away why.

Uncle Ovid was sitting at the table getting his first cup of coffee, and, my goodness, he looked fine. I could just barely remember him looking that way, long ago, when I first came to visit him. His face was all pink and shining behind the white moustache, and his shirt was very white, and the coat with the padded right shoulder was brushed, and there was a shine on his boots that reflected the lamplight like a mirror. He was very cheerful and kept making little jokes, and Mr. Washington gave me my breakfast, and all of a sudden I felt fine, too.

194

The kitchen was warm from the stove and familiar and comfortable by the old yellow lamplight, and the ham made everything smell wonderful. Mr. Washington kept on working at the range, and Uncle Ovid told me about other Nationals he had seen, like in 1902, when Sioux was returned the winner for the second time, after running the National's greatest heat in three hours of freezing sleet. Mr. Hochwalt was there, Uncle Ovid said, and had written about it so I might read how it was, but he was there to tell me it was splendid. And he told me about La Besita, the last Llewellin to win, and how she ran in the ice with Brunswick Countess to find nine coveys and three singles. I sat there, fascinated, and Uncle Ovid said happily, "This is just like old times, isn't it, boy?"

"Yes, sir," I said, happily, too, and right then is when it stopped being like anything.

Algonquin coughed.

The cough started tearing at him, and he would not give in to it, but the immense cage of his ribs heaved and shuddered, and something in his throat made a choking sound, but Uncle Ovid did not look up or stop chuckling at a little joke he had just

195

made. I stopped eating and turned myself to stare at the dog with some terrible premonition, and he was looking straight at Uncle Ovid, and then I knew what was different. It was his eyes, not bitter anymore, not mocking or full of hate but aflame with triumph—*triumph*. The frigid spell cast over his heart all these years was burned away by the bright flame of victory, and the dark shadows were lighted up, and there was no more need for fury; the hard times were almost over, and he had made it safely; nothing could hurt him anymore, and you could see by the way he looked at Uncle Ovid that they had entered into a fatal pact.

I put my hands over my face with a frantic gesture and cried out something. Mr. Washington turned around from the range, and I saw in horror that his eyes were swollen and bloodshot and the tears had made long, clean streaks down his whiskery face. Then my grandfather came into the kitchen, tall and formal and austere and as coldly distant as a mountaintop, and no one had to tell me after that what was going to happen.

Uncle Ovid stood up, and I said, "Please, I don't want to go."

"You got a right," Uncle Ovid said firmly. "He was your dog, away back from the beginning. He was your dog by right, and now you got to stand by him."

"I don't want to go," I said. "Do I have to, Grandsir?"

Maybe he didn't hear me. He had buttoned his coat and was pulling on his gloves and saying names to himself like he was calling a roll. In the silence, I heard them, the magic rolling sound of the fabulous roster, conjuring up visions of triumphs in the past: High Valor and Stanford Lad and Blue Dan and Riptide and Roanoke and Prime Minister and all the rest, all slain before their time.

"All right," I said. "All right, then."

And when I got up, I said bitterly, in a way I never had talked to my elders before, "If you don't want to leave me anything."

Uncle Ovid did not seem to hear. Anyway, it was a foolish thing to say, because doing it this way he left me everything and did not keep any of it for himself.

There were only three horses, so Mr. Washington walked with the dogs, his own old setter and

Algonquin, walking slowly, for Algonquin's sake. Grandsir rode with the reins folded in his gloved hands, and Uncle Ovid rode a little ahead, smiling straight into the coming sunrise and holding before him the shotgun Lou Smith's daddy made for him, the lovely, graceful gun with the gold and silver all over it.

When we got as far as we were going, Uncle Ovid reined up, but he did not dismount and go to the dog and talk to him and put into him the reserves of his strength, because he needed them all himself, all there was left, and Algonquin didn't, not ever anymore. He just motioned, and Mr. Washington cast the old setter away and Algonquin went out all right, without coughing.

Mr. Washington's bitch did not move well anymore; she was breaking down behind and Algonquin went away out wide, but she kept on after him. Then, on the ridge, Algonquin had to stop and cough. It was awful to see, even from that far away, and the lame old bitch caught up to him, and, with him standing there retching, she moved past. You could see his head turn and his eyes show the yellow flame as she went by, and Uncle Ovid

199

gave a ghastly choking kind of a cry, but Algonquin would not let it be this way. He stopped coughing and plunged out, for ten seconds looking like he used to, high and wide and so handsome it made your throat ache. The bitch was making game, a little tentatively, and Algonquin swept up to her so fast I thought he would slam into her, but he didn't; he had the wonderful gallantry even when time was running out, and he bathed her in that spotlight of his own greatness to make her proud and happy, but she stumbled, and the bird flushed wild. Then he went on past her, in an absolutely scorching burst of speed, and fifty yards farther on he hit the covey, moving with that almost footless velocity that swung him in a long, graceful pinwheel when the scent stopped him. The sun was just fairly up beyond the hills, and there was not much color, just the blue sky and the spring-brown fields and Algonquin silhouetted on the hill, majestically in that one moment all that he ever was.

I tried to lag behind, but they waited until my horse came up even.

"There, boy," Uncle Ovid said. "You want to remember that. He has come all the way, and no dog ever touched him or came near to him, and there never was anything like that out there right this minute, because there never before was a dog like Algonquin."

He did not have to tell me; no one had to tell me anything about Algonquin. He was my dog, my first dog, and I knew more about him than anyone else dared know. He stood there, and he knew how it was. I could tell from the way he stood that he was speaking to the birds for the last time now. They were alarmed by the feeling in the air, but he was pouring out the final eloquence of his genius, saying: *Fare thee well, little brothers; be thee beautiful for me one time more, and be at peace, for it is not thee who shall be slain today; put out the candles of thy alarm and look upon me one time more—thou shalt not see my like again, little brothers, not like me who loved thee. Look one time more into my eyes, then say farewell and rise together and fly strongly in a pattern that makes a unity of all of us: of earth and sky and men, and thee and me.*

And my Uncle Ovid dismounted then, and I looked straight ahead, crying, and he walked up to where Algonquin was on point. The birds burst beautifully, like a skyrocket, and instead of shooting them, he shot Algonquin in the head.

Afterward, he picked up the dog, and the shotgun lay there, the one Lou Smith's daddy made with all the gold, and I wouldn't touch it, and Grandsir wouldn't even look at it, so it was just left there, and all the way back Uncle Ovid carried the dead dog, and I walked behind him, weeping, and the horses followed us, and Grandsir rode off across the field, with the old setter following him, and Mr. Washington walked behind all of us, saying over and over, in a strong, calm voice, "Now I lay me down to sleep, I pray the Lord my soul to keep."

IV

*"Behold the consuming rage," Grandsir had said.
And all the rest is ashes. That is how it was.*

13

ON THE WAY HOME, we did not talk much until the train was away from the prairie country and safely into the moraine, where the hills are very abrupt and there are many lakes, all hard, dark-blue-colored, and the marshes stretch away between the hills for miles, but the grainfields are very small and tidy. We changed trains in the city, and there was a while between, so Grandsir and I walked up the ramp from the depot and looked around. A man wearing golden earrings was selling balloons on the corner, and across the street in a park the kids were playing baseball.

"Well, boy," Grandsir said. "Now you know."

"Yes, sir," I said.

"A man has only so much time," Grandsir said. "He has a right to make up his own mind how he wants to spend the time he is allowed."

"Yes, sir," I said.

"Presently," Grandsir said, "we will go out and find a puppy. Maybe an Irish setter."

"Irish setters don't win field trials, do they?" I asked. "I mean, you are not running much danger of getting a great dog, are you?"

Grandsir pursed his lips a moment.

"No," he said. "Not much danger."

"Then an Irish setter would be nice," I said.

The man who wore golden earrings began to sing in a liquid tenor voice.

Grandsir asked, "Do you know anyone who maybe would rather have a new bicycle or something when we get home?"

I said, "No, sir. Bicycles are for young boys."

"Yes," Grandsir said after a moment. "To be sure."

Then we were home, and because no one mentioned those times again, I became busy with other things. I went back to school and settled down with youngsters my own age again, the familiar, city kind of youngsters who never would have to worry about what I had worried about and did not know anything about that kind of life, so I was spared explaining anything. Most of them were wonderfully ignorant about the important things, and hardly any of them knew anything about bird dogs, or cared, because they were spending all their time finding out about athletics and training rules and girls. It was a great relief, and after a while I forgot very easily many of the things I had learned so hard, but I did not ever get another bicycle.

It could not have been past midsummer that I came home, though, and found Grandsir glaring at a handful of letters and looking very stern and worried. I asked him if they were about Uncle Ovid, but Grandma said, "Tend to your own knitting, sir."

She talked that way a considerable part of the time, but I had heard her enough to know when she wasn't fooling, and this was one of the times. As I said, though, I was very busy and did not actually think about it very much until Grandsir packed his bag quite suddenly one day and got on a train for the Old Place. As I said, it was the middle of the summer, and there wasn't any shooting or anything. That was what puzzled me first; then I settled down enough to figure it must be about Uncle Ovid, and I was just stubborn enough to want to go along, but he wouldn't let me.

At the station, Grandsir said something to Grandma about how it was time someone took the old man in hand. I guess, though, that it must have been a little bit past time, because Grandma heard from Grandsir by telegram just a day or two afterward and was very upset. I asked her if there was something wrong with Uncle Ovid, and Grandma started to get a certain expression on her face, then paused, and instead her face became very soft and gentle, and she said, "Ovid is all right now, boy."

At first, they would not let me go to the funeral, but when the time came, I did. They thought perhaps I might not be very good when I saw Uncle Ovid that way in the church, but they couldn't fool me; that wasn't Uncle Ovid there. I knew better, but they fooled a lot of people.

When we came back from the church, the house was full of people, not from our town but from all the distant places, with the soft sound of travelers in their voices, men I had always seen with their eyes squinted against the sun, with whistles in their hands and fresh dust on their boots, looking new and strange, now, in the black suits.

They were a little uneasy with the womenfolk around, especially Grandma, from the way they kept bowing and making flowery compliments, but when they drifted away from the parlor into the library, they relaxed and looked at the pictures standing there in their frames above the bookcases, and one of them said he allowed it was a pity and a shame for a man to break his heart that way over a dog.

"That's purely the truth," said another, "and I reckon the only thing keeps it such a seldom sin is that not many of us have that kind of a dog—nor that kind of a heart."

There was a picture of Algonquin in the library now, opposite the one of High Valor, and he was splendid in it, tall and white and proud, proud, proud, with the dark head turned a little and the yellow eyes looking out, not at you, but beyond you, forever, lighted with the cold, white light that always glowed around him and was the color of grief and victory.

"Now they have all passed away," the first man said. "And we are safe, finally. The judge is right, how no one cares that much about dogs anymore."

And I guess he was.

Anyway, we didn't go west that year or the next year, and finally I asked Grandsir if perhaps we could not go back.

"You can," he said and looked at me from beneath those bushy brows. "But if you are wise, you'll wait until you are a little older."

I did not see why it mattered; I could always go back again.

"No," Grandsir said. "Just one time more."

That was a strange thing for him to say. We were in the library, and suddenly I became conscious of the old feeling, of the power and magic, and I looked up at the picture of Algonquin and the sweat started wet in my clenched hands, because I felt I was very close to something for maybe the last time.

"Sir," I said, "why did my uncle always live alone?"

There was a silence that stretched out interminably, and I thought for a moment that Grandsir would not answer me. But at length he said, "As a young man, Ovid was disappointed in love."

I did not say anything at all.

Grandsir said, "Nothing is left now, not of the house or the grounds or the trees or anything. Except the stone. Did you know?"

"No," I said.

"It is real marble, like you buy for your kinsmen. Ovid had them carry it from Italy, so that the man who carved angels might come and cut upon it the word that was a name."

I said, "Algonquin."

"That's all," Grandsir said. "Nothing else is left."

Whitman CLASSICS and ANTHOLOGIES

Black Beauty

Little Women

Heidi

Heidi Grows Up

Tom Sawyer

Huckleberry Finn

The Call of the Wild

Treasure Island

Alice in Wonderland

The Wonderful Wizard of Oz

Famous Fairy Tales

Algonquin: The Story of a Great Dog

Tales of Poe

SHORT STORY COLLECTIONS

A Batch of the Best (Stories for Girls)

Like It Is (Stories for Girls)

Shudders

Golden Prize

That's Our Cleo! *(New)*

Way Out *(New)*

Whitman NOVELS FOR GIRLS

Spirit Town

Gypsy From Nowhere

The Family Name

True to You

Practically Twins

Make-Believe Daughter

The Silver Seven

Bicycles North! *(New)*

Whitman ADVENTURE and MYSTERY Books

THE TRIXIE BELDEN SERIES
16 Exciting Titles

MEG MYSTERIES
The Disappearing Diamonds
The Secret of the Witch's Stairway
The Treasure Nobody Saw
The Ghost of Hidden Springs
The Mystery of the Black-Magic Cave
Mystery in Williamsburg

DONNA PARKER
Takes a Giant Step
On Her Own
Mystery at Arawak
Special Agent

KIM ALDRICH MYSTERIES
Miscalculated Risk
Silent Partner
The Deep Six *(New)*
The Long Shot *(New)*

TELEVISION FAVORITES
Lassie
Lost in the Snow
Trouble at Panter's Lake
The Mod Squad
Hawaii Five-O
Family Affair

SPORTS AND ADVENTURE STORIES
Throw the Long Bomb! (Football)
Basket Fever (Basketball)
Cellar Team (Baseball)
Drag Strip Danger (Racing)
Divers Down! (Undersea Adventure)

TEE-BO, THE TALKING DOG
2 Titles in This Rollicking New Series